SEPTEMBER
SECRET

GW00746637

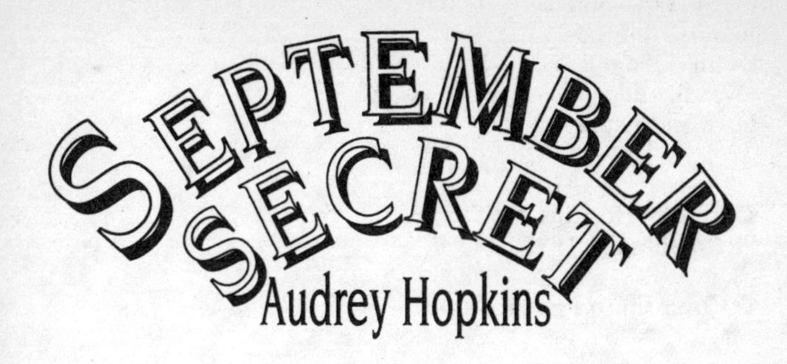

Audrey Hopkins

Scripture Union
130 City Road, London EC1V 2NJ.

By the same author
Joanna's Journey
Double Trouble
Over the Edge
Love and Laura

First published 1995

ISBN 0 86201

British Library Cataloguing-in-Publication Data.
A catalogue record for this book is available from the British Library.

Phototypeset by Intype, London
Printed and bound in Great Britain by Cox & Wyman Ltd, Reading.

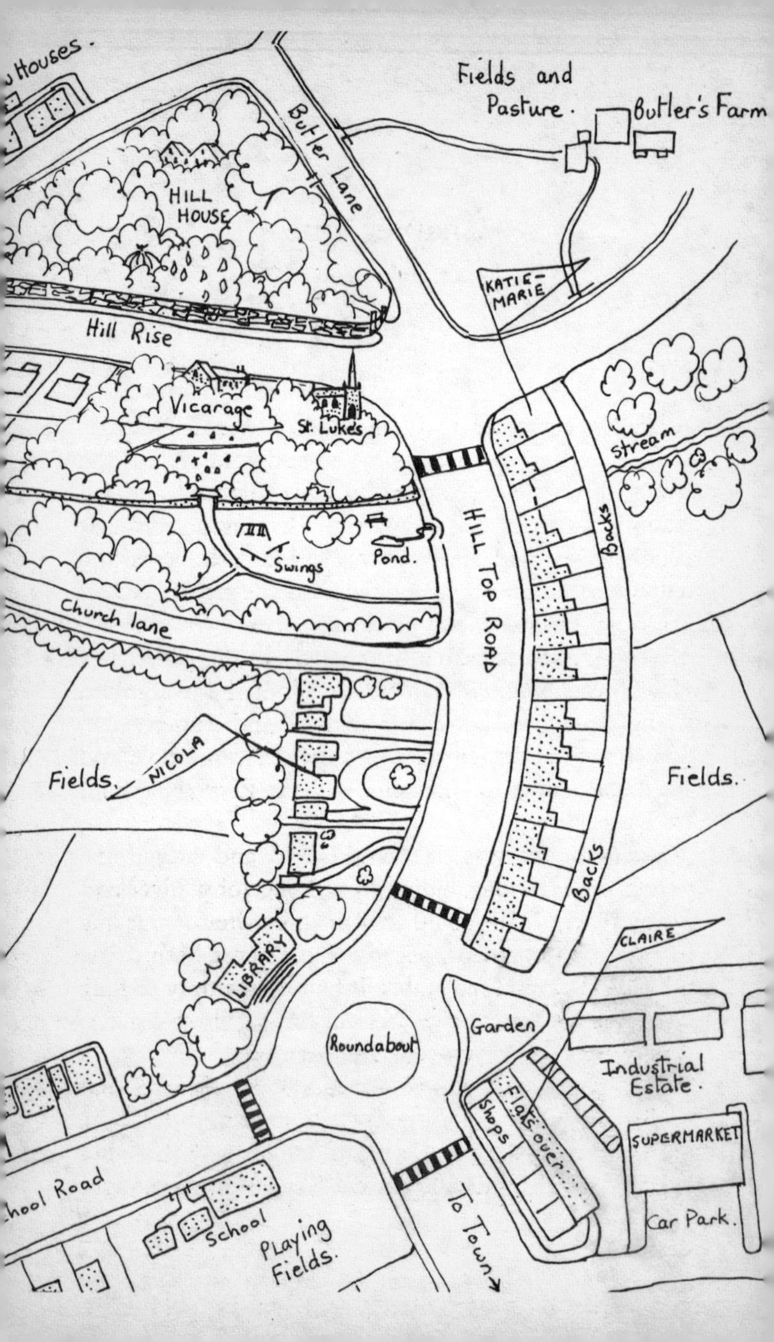
Houses.
Fields and Pasture.
Butler's Farm
Butler Lane
HILL HOUSE
KATIE-MARIE
Hill Rise
Vicarage
St. Luke's
Stream
Swings
Pond.
HILL TOP ROAD
Backs
Church lane
NICOLA
Fields.
Fields.
Backs
CLAIRE
LIBRARY
Roundabout
Garden
Industrial Estate.
Shops
Flats over
SUPERMARKET
Car Park.
School Road
School
Playing Fields.
To Town

Chapter One

Abigail stood at her bedroom window. Across Hill Rise the tall trees were tipped with red and gold and, as she watched, a shower of crinkled leaves danced and fell behind the high, red brick wall. It was a sign that summer was over, and that was sad, but she loved the colours of autumn that looked as if the trees were on fire when the sun shone on them.

Abigail liked to watch the changes in the gardens of Hill House. She made up stories about the overgrown triangle of green between Hill Rise and Butler Lane. Sometimes she imagined it was the African jungle and she was looking for the source of the River Nile with Dr Livingstone.

Sometimes it was *Treasure Island* and herself the young Jim Hawkins, hiding from Long John Silver and his pirate crew. She could only imagine what it was like in Hill House gardens, because she'd never been there, not that she could remember. It had been empty so long that even the front drive, behind the big double gates, was overgrown with weeds and brambles.

Hill House itself was almost hidden by the trees and bushes and all she could see of the summer house was the rusty cockerel that once told which way the wind blew. It always pointed east now and Abigail thought it must be stuck, neglected like the rest of the property. It was only in winter that parts of the house could be seen from her window, the bits that rose above the rhododendrons and laurels that surrounded it. Hill House looked so lonely when the trees were bare.

In summer, all that poked above the leafy trees was the steep roof with its tall twisted chimneys and sometimes, when the sun caught the glass in the gable window, it was fun to imagine who might have lived up there, in the roof, and make up stories about them.

Abigail could just remember people living in Hill House. She could remember a snowy winter's night and being carried up the long drive to sing carols to old Mr Lyle. If she thought really hard she could picture a big room with a log fire and a lot of red candles, but it might have been a picture on a Christmas card and not a memory of Hill House at all.

'Abby! Abigail! Breakfast!'

Reluctantly, Abigail left the window and picked up her school bag. Summer was over and it was time to go back to school and work. Abigail liked school and enjoyed learning, but it was always sad when the long, lazy summer days were over.

'Come on, Abby, hurry up! I'm going to school today!'

Abigail grinned as she ran down the wide stairs. That was Daniel!

'Why is he so excited? School's boring!'

That was Matthew!

Mrs Dutton was timing eggs at the cooker when Abigail went into the kitchen.

'Put your school bag in the hall, Abigail,' she said without turning round. 'And eat your cornflakes.'

Abigail grinned at her brothers. Mum always knew

everything, even that she still had her bag on her shoulder! Dad said that Mum had eyes in the back of her head, especially when he tried to creep into the kitchen with mud on his gardening boots!

It was the beginning of September and the first day of a new school year. Abigail's brother, Daniel, was starting school for the first time and he had been looking forward to it for weeks.

'Hurry up, Abby!' he cried, stuffing cornflakes into his already full mouth and dribbling milk down his chin.

Abigail ignored him, like someone who was *twice* as old as he was should, but he had such a lovely smile on his round face that she couldn't ignore him for long. She did love her little brother.

'There's plenty of time, Daniel,' she said. 'Wipe your chin!'

Daniel picked up the white linen square and scrubbed at his lips.

'Is it off?'

Abigail nodded and poured milk from the silver jug onto her cornflakes.

Matthew sighed. He was eight and liked school, as long as he was out on the field with Mr Jones and a football.

'I don't know why he's so excited,' he moaned. 'Most of the time you have to sit at the table and write!'

'At this table we eat!' Mr Dutton said, 'we don't write with spoons so eat your cornflakes!' There was silence then, as the family tucked into boiled eggs and toast, and Mr Dutton winked at Matthew, to show him that he wasn't really angry.

The vicarage kitchen was large and draughty, which didn't matter too much on a sunny September morning.

In winter time, Mr Dutton opened the fire door on the old range and let the hot coals warm the room.

Abigail knew that two of her friends had breakfast on a specially designed bar with stools and that Claire had her toast on her knee in front of the TV, which would be fun, but the white embroidered tablecloth, the matching cups and plates and the silver tea-set gave her a cosy feeling inside. It was a family 'thing' to eat at the table with linen napkins and a jam spoon in the pretty pot with flowers on the lid.

The silver service had been Gramps' and his father's before him. It had been used every day since it was made. Gramps was Mr Dutton's father and had come to live at the vicarage when Gran died. He lived in a little 'Grandad' flat that had been made out of the laundry room, the outside toilet and the conservatory. Gramps had his own bed-sitting room and a bathroom and Mrs Dutton took all his meals into him. He had his own kettle for making tea and a tin full of ginger biscuits to give to his grandchildren when they popped in. Daniel was always popping in.

Abigail's friend, Nicola, told everyone that it was 'posh' at the vicarage, after she had stayed the night, but it wasn't! All the things were used and well worn and it was just what Abigail's family 'did'! She could imagine her Gramps face if he'd seen Nicola stick her buttery knife into the marmalade!

The vicarage stood to the north of the parish church of St. Luke with the front gate on Hill Rise. It was a rosy-red brick building with ivy all the way up the front walls.

The rooms were big, the ceilings high and the wood-work dark and shiny. Mrs Dutton used a lot of polish and was always saying that she wished they lived in a modern house with white plastic windows and doors, but she didn't mean it!

Mr Dutton spent a lot of time in his study, writing his sermons and having parish meetings. It was in a corner and didn't get much sun so there was nearly always a fire in there. Sometimes, when it was really cold, the whole family gathered by the study fire to play Scrabble and other games instead of watching TV in the lounge, a huge room that was always draughty.

Abigail and her brothers had hot-water bottles in their beds and thick duvets to snuggle into. They had bed socks too, to warm their toes. Sometimes Abigail stayed at Nicola's house and never felt comfortable in her heated bedroom.

The vicarage had a wide staircase with a banister just right for sliding down. Mrs Dutton laughed and said that at least she didn't have to polish the mahogany rail but Mr Dutton frowned on the practice, with a twinkle in his eye. Abigail had seen him, more than once, sliding down when he thought no-one was looking!

After breakfast, the Duttons set off for Hill Top Primary School. Mrs Dutton went on ahead with Matthew and Daniel while Abigail waited by the pond for Katie-Marie.

Katie-Marie lived in the end house at the top of Hill Top Road and her dad saw her across it as he set off to work. The two girls always met at their special bench by the big oak. There was a piece of common land between Church Lane and the church itself and it was a meeting place for elderly gentlemen who sat on the benches chatting and ladies walking their dogs. For the children there was a small playground with two see-saws and a set of swings. Just by the side of the road was a pond that was filled by a tiny stream that ran along by the church wall and there was a big pipe that disappeared under Hill Road to take away the overflow. Sometimes the ducks decided to cross the road and drivers had to be careful.

Abigail fed the ducks while she waited for Katie-Marie, sorting out their squabbles and making sure every one of them had something from her bag of stale bread.

'Don't be so greedy!' she said to a very fat duck who was bullying the others. 'We don't want any of *that* kind of behaviour, thank you very much!'

'You sound just like Mrs Clarke!' a voice said, right by her elbow.

'Katie-Marie Griggs, you made me jump!' Abigail cried, shaking out the last of the crumbs and dropping the bag in the litter bin before hugging her friend. 'I've missed you! Did you have a nice time?'

Katie-Marie had been to visit her real father and his new wife, and had been away for most of the six weeks holiday.

'It was great, and Sally's really nice, but I'm glad to be home! I missed Mum and Dad, and Stacey's *really* grown!'

Katie-Marie had a baby step-sister and was very proud of her.

Further down Hill Top Road, on the same side as the pond, was Nicola's house, and she was sitting on the front wall waiting for them.

'I wish holidays were longer!' she grumbled, jumping off the wall and skipping to get into step with the others. 'I hate school!'

'No you don't!' Abigail said. 'You like it as much as

I do. It's only that it's Monday morning!'

'It isn't! I don't care what day it is. I've ridden Patches every day, except when we went to Majorca, and he'll miss me! Hi Kit-Kat!'

'Hi Nick!' Katie-Marie answered.

'Here we go again!' Abigail sighed. Her two friends were always teasing each other with nicknames.

Claire was at the school gates. They could see her as they rounded the corner by the library. She was jigging up and down and waving her arms. She had her back to them and was still bouncing when Abigail tapped her on the shoulder.

'Oooh! What? Abby Dutton, you scared me!'

'What *are* you doing, Claire?' Nicola said, her hands on her hips and her head shaking from side to side.

Claire had two orange sponges pressed against her ears, with wires that disappeared into her pocket.

'I got it at the holiday camp, first prize in the disco-dancing competition. Isn't it ACE!'

Abigail frowned at the little red personal stereo that Claire took out and held up for them to admire.

'You'd better put it away before we go in,' she said. 'The teachers will take it off you!'

'Some of them would. I wonder who we'll have?' Kate-Marie sighed as they reached the side entrance.

'Somebody nice, I hope!' Nicola said, remembering last year and Mrs Clarke. 'Mrs Clarke was really grumpy!'

All the school stood in the hall for Assembly. They sang 'Morning has broken' and prayed for a happy and productive school year, then Mr Johnson read out the lists and asked the form teachers to collect their classes and take them to their rooms.

Nicola sighed with relief. It wasn't Mrs Clarke after all! They had a new teacher, Miss Newton, and they were to be called 6N.

'She looks nice!' Katie-Marie whispered.

'I hope she's as nice as she looks!' Claire said as they found four desks together by the windows.

Abigail nodded, her dark eyebrows meeting as she frowned.

'What's the matter?' Claire asked.

'It's Matthew. He's gone with Mrs Clarke and I'll bet he's in trouble by home-time! He was hoping for Mr Jones.'

'He'll have him for football won't he? All the boys have games with Mr Jones.' Nicola said from the desk behind her.

'I'd forgotten that,' Abigail nodded. 'But he'll still have Mrs Clarke for most of the day. Poor Matthew!'

'Good morning everybody,' Miss Newton said.

'Good morning Miss Newton,' the class chanted.

For the next hour they were busy with registers, address checks, dinner numbers and timetables (so they'd know when to bring swimming things and PE kit). Then new books were given out and named ready for each lesson.

Abigail liked everything organised. She liked to stick a little coloured disc on each of her blue exercise books: red for arithmetic, green for writing, orange for spelling, purple for science and so on. The children were allowed to stick pictures on their books too, and she already had some ideas for hers.

When everything had been done, Miss Newton asked everyone to stand up and talk about their interests in a few sentences, starting with the first name on the register.

'I like to get to know my class straight away,' she said. 'Martin Allsop?'

'I like football and computer games.'

'Is that all, Martin?'

He nodded. Martin never did say very much.

'Abigail Dutton. Is it Abigail or Abby?'

Abigail said that she didn't mind either and took a deep breath to stop her voice from shaking – she hated being 'on show' and always bent her head when she stood up. She was taller than anyone else in the class, even the boys! She didn't mind telling stories but hated talking about herself.

'I live at the vicarage on Hill Rise. I have two brothers and I like to play board games with them. I like reading and making up stories.'

'Thank you, Abigail. Do you write your stories down?' Miss Newton asked.

'Sometimes.'

'Good! Perhaps you'll read some to the class one day? Who's next?'

Claire talked about music – pop music. She even took out her red stereo to show the class and Abigail held her breath, sure that Miss Newton would take it and put it in her desk drawer until the end of term. Mrs Clarke had done that with Clancy Mason's lucky troll when she saw him sitting on Clancy's desk.

Claire didn't have any brothers and sisters. Sometimes she was glad, like when her friends had to look after theirs. Sometimes she felt quite lonely when there was no-one at home.

Claire lived in a flat above the shops and had her own key because her Mum didn't get home until six.

'I'm going to be a dancer,' Katie-Marie said. 'I go to dancing school and when I'm twelve I'm going to go on points, in blocked shoes. When I'm sixteen I'm going to get a scholarship to a ballet school, if I'm good enough!'

After Nicola had described her horse, Patches, gymkhanas and point-to-point meetings, Miss Newton was thrilled!

'What a talented lot I have,' she said. 'A writer, a pop star, a ballerina and an olympic horsewoman, all in one class. I wonder what other talents we have?'

Everybody looked at the four friends and it was easy to imagine what they would be when they grew up. Abigail was tall, like her dad, with very dark hair and eyes, like her mum. She was always careful with words, never saying hurtful or silly things. Abigail was always very serious and hard-working in class. She told wonderful stories in the playground, leaving the heroine in dangerous situations just as the bell went, then everybody had to wait for the next episode!

Claire was short, plumpish and always had a huge grin on her freckled face. Her hair was carroty-red and curly and it bounced when she danced and sang. Everything about Claire was bouncy! It was easy to imagine her bouncing on the stage on Top of the Pops!

Katie-Marie was very pretty. She was just the right height and just the right weight for a dancer. She had a pointed chin, brown hair in thick plaits and long hands and feet. When she moved, everything fitted, as though somebody had worked out the steps. Katie-Marie was always the star at school concerts.

Nicola had a long blond ponytail and she had a habit of tossing her head when something upset her. She stamped her feet too, when she was really angry! Nicola laughed a lot and was always jumping on and off walls, vaulting gates and running. She never *walked* anywhere. Her dad was always telling her to 'stop galloping about!' Her mum said that when Nicola came downstairs she sounded like a herd of elephants!

After hearing about stamp collecting, scrambling on a mountain bike, being a Brownie and learning Tai Kwan Do, they came to the end of the list.

It was Simon Wardle, who was the bad boy of the class and always getting into mischief! Everybody laughed when he said that he wanted to be a clown because he did have a funny face and sticky-out ears, but Simon really meant it. He knew a lot about clowns, about each one being different.

'Every clown has his own face,' Simon said. 'And no-one else can use it. I'm going to have my face registered when I'm ready. I'm going to be a 'white-faced' clown.'

Simon explained that clown faces are painted on egg-shells, registered in a book and stored in a special room.

'It's like a copyright,' Miss Newton said. 'And that's a word you can all look up in the dictionary. That's really interesting, Simon, and we could all design a clown's face next Art lesson.'

'Can we be clowns in Drama?' Simon asked.

'There's a song about clowns! I've heard it,' Claire squealed, bouncing up and down in her seat. 'We could write poems and put music to them with the keyboard!'

'We could do a clown dance, and somebody could be Harlequin and Columbine,' Katie-Marie added, hoping it was her that was chosen to dance in a beautiful ballet dress.

And that's how the History project began! Miss Newton thought it was an excellent idea because they could use the project in a lot of their lessons.

'But it has to be more than juggling, acrobatics and painting faces!' Miss Newton said.

'I'd like to find out how it all began. Weren't jesters clowns?' Abigail asked quietly.

'They were, and William Shakespeare had them in his plays. It looks as if Abigail will find out WHEN . . . what about calling our project the History of Clowns?'

'Can we do more than clowns? I'd like to do Ballet?' Katie-Marie said.

'And Music?'

'And Pantomimes.'

There were hands up everywhere and the classroom was buzzing with enthusiasm.

'It had better be a History of Entertainment, then everybody can find out about their own interests, yes?'

'Yes!'

It was going to be an exciting year with Miss Newton!

'She's really nice,' Abigail said as they walked home. 'Really nice!'

Chapter Two

Jilly was tired. They had walked all the way from the bus station and although Grandad carried the heavy suitcases, there was still her sleeping bag to carry, as well as her own sports bag full of clothes, some shopping and the little picnic stove.

Grandma was puffing and panting by the time they reached the pond and crossed the grass to the nearest bench.

'I don't remember Hill Top Road being so steep!' she gasped, putting the carrier bags down to rest her arms.

'You were six years younger, Sarah, and thinner!' Grandad said, winking at Jilly. 'The ducks are still as fat as ever!'

'I suppose the local children are feeding them crisps! They used to love the bread from my kitchen,' Grandma told her.

'Is it much further, Grandad?' Jilly asked him.

'Past the church and round the corner then it's just a hop and a skip to the back gate!'

'It's like coming home,' Grandma sighed, getting to her feet and picking up the bags. 'I've carried a lot of shopping up this hill!'

Jilly looked this way and that as they trudged on, trying to remember the place. She knew she had been here when she was little. Mum and Dad had brought her in the summer holidays and at Easter, but nothing looked familiar.

It was only as they were passing the big double gates that Jilly remembered Hill House.

'The summer house!' she cried.

'That's it, Jilly. I knew you'd remember. You used to play in the summer house while I tidied the gardens.'

'I remember,' Jilly nodded. 'But people lived in the house then, an old man with white hair.'

'Old Mr Lyle,' Grandma sighed. 'He was a gentleman! I always felt at home at Hill House, even though I was only the housekeeper and cook.'

'Only? What do you mean *only*. You were the best housekeeper in the country!'

Jilly's grandparents, Mr and Mrs Potts, had worked for Mr Lyle since they were young. Mrs Potts started out as a maid, then cook and finally housekeeper when Mrs Lyle died and Mr Lyle was alone in the house. Mr Potts was the chauffeur and later, when Mr Lyle became an invalid and never left the house, he became the handyman and gardener. It was while he was the chauffeur that he had fallen in love with the maid, and married her. He had lived up at the top of Butler Lane then, and used to start work early so he'd had breakfast in the kitchen at Hill House. He'd first seen Sarah Higgins when she'd come for clean water for the hall floor and it had been love at first sight!

It was quite a romantic story and Jilly never tired of hearing about it. Mr Lyle let the newlyweds have the rooms above the coach house and they made them into a comfortable home. Jilly's dad had been born above the coach house and had lived there too, until he went into the army and married Mum.

'Here we are!'

Jilly stopped thinking about Dad and Mum. It made her miserable, wondering whether Dad had found work and somewhere for them to live, and she had to dump the sleeping bag and find a hanky to blow her nose rather quickly.

'Mind where you put that, Jilly! You'll be needing it to sleep in, tonight. It'll be cold and we mustn't light a fire or someone will see the smoke!'

Jilly picked up the sleeping bag in its canvas cover and watched as Grandad fiddled with the back gate. There was a big padlock and chain on the sliding bolt but Grandad was working at the other side, near the hinges.

'Is there anybody about?' he whispered.

'Not a soul!' Grandma said. 'So there's no need to whisper. Just hurry up!'

Jilly's eyes were wide with astonishment when she saw Grandad lift the gate right off its hinges and push it open over the tangle of grass and roots that were growing behind it.

'Inside, quick!' he said.

'How did you do that?' Jilly asked.

'Your Grandad knows that gate like the back of his hand, Jilly. He's mended it often enough – and it was him that put the chain on when we left.'

Grandma and Grandad Potts had come to live with Jilly and her mum and dad when old Mr Lyle died and Hill House was all closed up. It was a sad time for them, because it had been their home for years and because the lovely old house had been emptied and the windows boarded up. Jilly could remember Grandad talking about it when they first came to Radley, where Jilly lived.

Jilly's dad was the boss of a haulage company, with a fleet of trucks that travelled all over Europe. Her mum was the firm's secretary and their house was right next to the depot, so there was always somebody there when Jilly got home from school.

It was a nice house with four bedrooms and there was plenty of room for Grandma and Grandad. It was lovely, all being together. Grandma was happy because she still had somebody to cook for and look after, and Grandad pottered about in the garden and made the flowers grow. It was a very happy family, until it happened.

Jilly didn't realise anything was wrong until the end. Mum and Dad had been just the same and she still had her piano lessons and the weekly treat to Water World with its five pools and water slides. Then Dad told her they had to move and tried to explain why. First, there was a fire at the depot and Dad had to borrow a lot of money to rebuild and replace the ruined trucks. Then people stopped hiring the trucks because somebody else could do the job cheaper. Half the drivers left because they were offered better pay, and finally the bank asked for all their money back, at least that's what Dad said. Suddenly they hadn't anything, not even a house, and it was awful!

'Now then Jilly, here's where we used to live. Do you remember now?'

Jilly didn't remember this bit at all. They had walked in single file between overgrown bushes and weeds and had emerged into a cobbled courtyard. The coach house had been converted when cars replaced coaches and the ground floor was a row of three garages with 'up and over' doors. One of the doors was open and the garage full of wood and rusty metal. The staircase to the upper floor was on the end of the building, on the outside, and it was overgrown with a creeping plant. There were brambles at the bottom, full of juicy black-berries and Grandad pulled them aside to clear a way.

'Now be careful!' he warned. 'Brambles can give you a nasty scratch. Have you got the key, Sarah?'

'I have, and keys to the big house too! I never meant to keep the spare set,' she explained to Jilly, who had gasped when she saw the keys. 'I didn't steal them, Jilly. I used to carry the house keys on a dog-lead clip fastened to my pinny strings. The spare set lived in my best handbag and I forgot they were there. We'd been with you five years before I realised I had them!'

'It's a good job you have too! I wouldn't want to *break* into the place. I wouldn't want to do any damage.'

There were four rooms in all, a living room, a small kitchen and a bedroom with a bathroom leading from it. They were all empty except for a small square table and a little three-legged stool.

'There's nothing here!' Jilly said softly, and a big lump grew in her throat.

'There isn't now, but there will be!' Grandad said. 'Grandma's got curtains in the suitcase and once they're up we can have candles on the table and a bite to eat.'

'There's nowhere to sit,' Jilly mumbled, and two large tears rolled down her cheeks. 'And I'm scared!'

'Now, Jilly, there's no need to be scared. We'll all stay together in this room until we get sorted out so you'll not be on your own!' Grandma said.

'But what will we sleep on?' Jilly asked, staring at the bare wooden floor.

'I've got your plastic blow-up air bed in one of the cases, and me and Grandad will manage, just for tonight. We'll sort something out, you'll see!'

'And there's a little stool, just your size! Come on Gran – get those curtains up while I go and turn on the water, that's all we need for now!' Grandad disappeared into the kitchen and through a door that led down a wooden staircase to the first garage.

Grandma gave her a cuddle.

'We'll be all right, Jilly.'

'But you can't sleep on the hard floor, Grandma!' Jilly sobbed.

'Come on, lovey, it's not that bad. We'll soon have the place like home. I'll sit on this soft suitcase, wrap myself in my old travelling rug and lean on Grandpa! He's nice and comfy.'

'It'll never be like home,' Jilly wailed. 'Home is my lovely bedroom and all my things! It's all gone!'

'It's only 'things' that have gone, Jilly. We've still got each other and we'll all be together again soon, you'll see. We've got soup and fresh bread, a lovely currant cake and a roof that doesn't leak!'

'We've got a lot more than that!' Grandpa called from somewhere down below. 'Come and give me a hand!'

He was half way down the stairs that led from the kitchen and Jilly and Grandma trod very carefully on the creaking boards.

It was dark, down in the garage, and at first Jilly couldn't see anything, but as her eyes got used to the gloom she could just make out some darker shapes.

'What is it?' she whispered.

'Treasure!' Grandad said mysteriously as he switched on his torch.

'Well I never!' Grandma cried. 'It's all the garden furniture!'

There were two old-fashioned deck chairs with striped canvas seats, a fold-away lounger with plastic webbing, a small wrought iron table, painted black with four chairs to match and a small white box, insulated to keep things cold.

'My word! I used to put drinks in that, for the garden when Mr Lyle had guests. That's when he was younger, of course. I haven't seen these things for years!' Grandma said. 'Weren't they kept in the garden shed?'

'They were, but they're here now, and look at this!'

Jilly and Grandma followed the torch beam into the far corner where it lit up a rusty object that looked like a fancy chimney pot.

'That's a paraffin stove, Jilly, and its got a good bit of wick left. Once I've been down to the shops we'll be warm and cosy, as well as comfortable!' Grandad said. 'I'll bet there's more hiding away down here!'

It didn't take long to carry the things upstairs. Grandad put the wooden table in the kitchen, arranging the wrought iron set by the window so that they could look out onto the courtyard and garden beyond when they were eating. The paraffin stove was put in the fireplace.

'The chimney'll get rid of the smelly fumes and there won't be any smoke if we keep the wick trimmed. I used this in my garden shed, Jilly. It's a good little burner!'

'I wonder why these things weren't sold?' Grandma said.

'They took the bits that were worth something, Sarah, all the lovely antiques. I heard he'd left a will – everything to be sold and put in trust for his brother's boy, wherever he is!'

Grandad left them to organise the curtains and supper while he went to buy paraffin and by the time he got back things did seem a little better.

'I could've done with a sweeping brush!' Grandma complained. 'I never thought to tell you to get one!'

'Plenty of time for that tomorrow. We can open all the windows to let the dust out, You don't want to be brushing up the dust while we're inside!'

Jilly had a sort of bed to sleep on and the stove worked, taking the chill off the air now that the sun had gone. It had been a bit scary while Grandad was away because it was so quiet here.

The bed and breakfast hostel had been right on a busy road and the traffic went up and down it all night. There were noises too, of people shouting and dogs fighting. It had been horrible!

After Grandma had put up the curtains, Jilly rubbed a clean circle on the dirty window and peered out at the tangle of bush and bramble that separated the coach house from the main building. The gravelled drive was almost hidden by weeds and the grass that had crept in from the sides. She couldn't see much of the house itself, just the side wall with its boarded up window and one of the front bays that jutted out on the corner.

'Come on, Jilly, time to light the candles and have a bite to eat,' Grandma said, drawing the thick curtains to stop the candlelight shining outside.

There was tomato soup simmering on the picnic stove, plastic mugs to put it in and bread rolls full of juicy ham on the table. It was almost like playing house! Jilly gulped again as she thought of Cathy next door at home and the old garden shed they had played in. Cathy's mum always let them have tea in there and they had a packing case table with a tea towel on top and two large paint tins to sit on; but that had been fun, just pretend and not real!

It was warm in the sleeping bag and quite comfortable on the lounger, as long as she didn't try to roll over! Jilly could hear Grandma and Grandad talking quietly, tucked under travelling rugs in the deck chairs. The one flickering candle made strange shadows on the faded wallpaper and a large spider crawled across the bare floor, right by her nose.

Jilly didn't feel scared at all! She felt safe in the house where Grandma and Grandad had been happy, safer than she had felt in the hotel and the bed and breakfast, even though the coach house was dirty and bare.

'We'll clean it all up tomorrow, won't we Grandma?' she asked quietly, propping herself up on her elbow to peer into the candle-glow.

'We will that, Jilly, till it's bright as a new pin!'

'And we're not doing anything *very* wrong, are we?'

Grandma and Grandad were silent for what seemed ages, then Grandad spoke.

'We shouldn't be here, Jilly, and that's no lie! We're trespassing, but we're not hurting anyone or doing any damage. Old Mr Lyle wouldn't mind, I'm sure.'

Trespassing! Jilly remembered seeing signs on her dad's property. 'TRESPASSERS WILL BE PROSECUTED', that meant being arrested and taken to court, and her stomach churned again as she thought how awful that would be!

Every night, from the moment she was able to talk, Jilly and her mum had said thank you to Jesus for the day, the family, and a safe night. Even when things went wrong and Mum and Dad had been too worried to talk to her, she still said her prayers and asked Jesus to help her dad sort things out. Jilly knew that prayers weren't always answered straight away and that, sometimes, the answers weren't the expected ones, but she was sure that Jesus would look after them all until things got back to normal.

'And forgive us our trespasses.'

That part of her prayer seemed to fit, there in a little room on somebody else's property, although Jilly knew it meant more than that; it meant all our wrong doings, including people being unkind to one another in a way that Jilly didn't always understand.

Jilly found it hard to get to sleep. She kept remembering all that had happened – watching all their furniture being loaded into a huge van, to be sold at auction; the FOR SALE notice being hammered into the front lawn, so beautifully cut in stripes by Grandad; the notice in the paper about 'Official Receivers' that everybody at school knew about and then how things got worse.

At first Grandad found a flat. There were two bedrooms and Jilly had a camp bed in with Mum and Dad. Then the landlord said they couldn't stay because Grandad hadn't said there was a child and if they stayed he would double the rent because there were two families in the flat, not one. He was a hateful man who shouted a lot.

Grandma and Grandad didn't get a big wage when they worked for Mr Lyle, because they lived there and had all their food provided. Their savings didn't last long when they had to pay hotel bills, and they lived in one for ages because they couldn't find another flat.

Six months after Dad lost the business they had to move out of the hotel and into a bed and breakfast place that the Social Services paid for. Dad couldn't rent a house because he didn't have a job and no-one would give him one because he didn't have a house or any references. He couldn't buy a house because he was bankrupt. Jilly didn't understand a lot of it, but everything seemed to be against them.

Her best friend, Cathy, didn't talk to her any more and the other girls at school turned up their noses at her new address. It was an awful place. They had to be out by nine in the morning and couldn't go back in until six at night. Grandma and Grandad sat in the library or on the benches in the shopping centre when it was raining, and in the park when it was fine. Jilly went to school, of course, and Mum and Dad went everywhere looking for work, but there was nothing in that area.

Things got worse! Somebody broke into their rooms and took the few precious things they had left and Grandma had a cough that wouldn't go away. Jilly took to playing truant. She hated people looking at her and whispering, then Dad decided to go and look for work in the city and Mum went with him. Jilly missed them terribly and spent a miserable six weeks holiday, crying herself to sleep most nights until Grandad decided to take things into his own hands and do something about it all.

'This is no way for a person to live!' he said one night when they were shivering in their one room. 'A man has a right to some dignity for his family!'

That's when it was decided that they would go home to Hill House. Grandad had been back to an old friend's funeral and knew that it was all boarded up and empty.

'We'll be better off there, until your dad sends for us, Jilly,' he said.

'What about school? The new term starts next week!'

'You can learn at home for a while. Your dad'll get a job soon so you won't miss much. We're not stopping here to be robbed, degraded and cold, and it's not even winter yet!'

'What about the pension?' Grandma asked. 'We'll need that to live on and you won't be able to change the address or the post office without letting on where we are!'

'We'll leave everything as it is and I'll get a bus every fortnight. We'll manage fine, Sarah,' Grandad said, kissing her worried frown away.

And that's how they came to be trespassing at Hill House. They had even less than they'd had at the bed and breakfast, but Jilly felt much happier. She dozed and thought about all the things they could do to make the place more comfortable. There could be more treasures down in the garage and there was the summer house she had remembered and the gardens to explore, so long as she wasn't seen . . . and there was nobody here to steal their things and make them miserable. She was sure everything was going to be all right.

'Forgive us our trespasses, as we forgive them that trespass against us, because it's wrong to break into someone else's property even if we do have a key, and it's wrong for people to be unkind to others. Please forgive us all,' she murmured as she finally fell asleep.

Chapter Three

It was Saturday morning. Abigail could tell it was the weekend because the smell of grilled bacon floated up the stairs from the kitchen. The Duttons always had a big cooked breakfast on Saturdays and Sundays.

Mr Dutton liked kidneys and the boys always asked for sausages and fried bread. Abigail liked potato cakes with a fried egg on top and Mrs Dutton's favourites were grilled tomatoes and button mushrooms. As Mrs Dutton was cooking all those things, everybody had a bit of everything, except the kidneys. Daniel didn't like them!

Abigail jumped out of bed, her tummy rumbling at the thought of all the lovely food, and ran to the window. The postman was just leaving and he looked up and waved, like he did most mornings.

Across Hill Rise the trees that surrounded Hill House were shrouded in mist. Sometimes that meant a miserable, rainy Saturday but Abigail was used to reading the signs. This mist was the wispy one that hung on the branches like cobwebs and it signalled another warm and sunny day.

She was smiling as she pulled on her jeans and found her favourite blue sweatshirt. These were her Saturday clothes, as were her blue and white striped socks and purple Kickers. There were things to be done on Saturdays and Abigail liked to have everything organised.

On her wall was a cork pin-board in a white frame and Abigail's lists were pinned on it with white-headed pins. She liked things that matched. There was a list of 'Things to take to school' and a weekly diary sheet to remind her of the daily happenings. There was a list of birthdays, so she didn't forget anybody and a page of things 'To think about' for when she had a moment spare.

Abigail checked her lists. There were no birthdays this week, and no special occasions to prepare for. Her school bag was already packed for Monday and her PE kit clean.

Once everything was organised and her bed made tidy she ran downstairs. Breakfast was a busy affair on Saturdays. All the food was kept warm in a heated trolley and each member of the family took a plate and served themselves. Abigail always helped Daniel, who was likely to drop a sausage and sometimes took too much. There were always seconds so it was silly to pile up a plate with food you might not be able to eat!

Once everyone had eaten their fill and the plates had been cleared away it was post time, then the Orders for Today were given out.

There was a letter for Abigail, from her penfriend in Wales. She'd met her on a holiday in Tenby and they'd written ever since. Michelle had been to Guernsey and there was a photograph of her on a lovely beach. The Duttons hadn't been on holiday that summer, because they were still paying for Gramps' little flat conversion.

Mr Dutton had three letters, all bills, and Daniel had an invitation to a birthday party.

'I never get anything!' Matthew complained.

'You never write to anybody! You can't expect to get when you don't give!' Abigail said.

Mr Dutton looked over his glasses at both of them.

'Nothing should be given for what could be got!' he said, then he smiled. 'But letters are a bit different. I certainly didn't write to these people, and look what I've got. Would you like one of mine, Matthew? We've got the same name so one of these *could* be yours!'

He held up the electricity bill but Matthew shook his head.

'That's not mine!' he grumbled.

Mrs Dutton sat down with a cup of coffee and the chores list.

'Now! Down to business,' she said, shuffling her bits of paper. 'Abigail – dusting the lounge, please, and shopping for Gramps if he needs anything. You could have a little chat too! Matthew – school shoes polished for Monday, please, then tidy the cupboard under the stairs. It looks as though there's been a tornado in there!'

'I couldn't find my football boots!' Matthew said.

'Daniel, flowers please!'

Daniel liked his job. Every Saturday morning he emptied the flower vases, the one in the hall and two in the lounge. He washed them out in the visitor's washroom by the front door and filled them with clean water. They were small vases and he could carry them easily, one at a time.

Then came the best bit. He was allowed to cut flowers and bits of shrubs from the gardens to fill the vases. He was very good at it and chose colours and shapes that looked nice together.

After Mrs Dutton had given out the chores it was time for news. Everyone was in a hurry on weekday mornings, had lunch at school and often had tea at different times, so Saturday morning was special, when they were all together with time to spare.

Sunday was special too but in a different way; Mr Dutton was in church very early then again later in the day. He visited people in the parish and was in church again for the evening service. Sunday was his busiest day.

Mrs Dutton had a letter from Aunty Carol. She had kept it until 'News' time because there was a photograph of a new cousin to pass round the table, and that was really good news! Uncle Robert had written the letter because Aunty Carol was still in the hospital with a new baby girl.

'She's called June, because that's when she was born!' Mrs Dutton read.

'She's lucky she wasn't born in March!' Mr Dutton said, and Daniel thought that was *very* funny!

Matthew had been picked for the first team and was very excited about it and Daniel had drawn a picture of the vicarage and coloured it with crayons.

'Miss Farrer said it was very good!' he said, proudly.

The picture was fastened on the fridge door with a magnet that looked like a slice of tomato and the picture of baby June went alongside it, held by a tiny teddy bear.

Abigail talked about the history project and how nice Miss Newton was, then Mr Dutton cleared his throat.

'Ahrr-um!' It was a signal and they all sat up straight and waited for him to begin.

Sometimes it was a funny story, one that he had made up or read in a magazine. Sometimes it was a riddle and nobody ever guessed it because he made those up too and the answers were silly, like 'What do you call a king who spends all his time cutting up cheese into very small pieces? . . . Alfred the Grater!' (That one had really made them groan!)

Some Saturdays, like this one, he had some news to tell.

'Did you know . . .?' he began in a mysterious voice.

'Know what?' they said, even more mysteriously and leaning forward to hear better.

'Hill House is for sale!'

'Is that all?' Matthew cried, slumping back into his seat and rolling his eyes.

'For sale?' Abigail felt her mouth dry up and she couldn't swallow. It wouldn't be the same with somebody living there. It wouldn't be *her* house anymore and she wouldn't be able to look at it because they would see her and think she was rude!

'Well, I suppose the house will be happy, having somebody living there again,' she said sadly.

'It won't, because Mr Yates wants it for building land. He's going to knock the house down and put thirty new houses on the land!' Mr Dutton said, slapping his knees as he sat back in his chair. 'That could mean a lot more people in my pews and more families for me to look after!'

Abigail felt sick, her lovely breakfast churning away inside as if it wanted to get out. Nicola's father was going to knock Hill House down and build thirty houses. Thirty! There wouldn't be bare branching fingers against the sky, and pale green buds in spring. There wouldn't be thick waving green above the blaze of rhododendrons and there wouldn't be the glorious red and gold of autumn. It was terrible.

'Has he bought it already?'

Abigail was thinking fast. Perhaps if she got up a

petition to save the trees?

Mrs Dutton put a comforting hand on Abigail's shoulder.

'I think it will be a great loss, it's a lovely old place. It would make a very nice retirement home, or a school? Perhaps someone else will buy it and keep it as it is.'

'I wish *we* could,' Abigail sighed.

'Us?' Mr Dutton sprang out of his chair and pulled out his pocket linings. 'With nothing in my pockets and all these bills?'

He sat down again and leaned forward.

'I'm afraid it's progress, Abby-Dabby. People need houses and houses need space. It's sad, but look on the bright side. A lot of people will have a nice place to live.'

Abigail knew she should care about people, but just then all she could think of was Hill House, and the thought of bulldozers and those huge iron balls that swung on cranes made her bite her lip to keep back the tears.

After she had done the dusting, Abigail went through into the flat. Gramps wasn't in his bed-sit so she knew he was in the conservatory.

'Hello Abby,' he said, looking up from his prize pelargoniums. 'You don't look too happy this morning!'

'No,' Abigail sighed, perching on a tall wicker stool by the plant table. 'Hill House is going to be knocked down!'

'Who's going to do that?'

'Nicola's Daddy. He's going to build a new estate. All I'll have to look at from my window is a lot of grey roofs!'

'Well that's a real shame. I used to play with one of the Lyle lads, when I was a nipper – that was . . . let's see – that was Alfred Lyle. He got married and went abroad somewhere!'

Abigail was going to ask about the inside of Hill House but Gramps had other things on his mind.

'I wonder if you'll go to the shops for me, Abby? There's a couple of things I need!'

Abigail smiled. There was always a couple of things that Gramps needed on a Saturday morning; his magazine about indoor plants and a packet of brown striped humbugs!

After her trip down to the shops, Abigail helped Gramps to tidy his little room, fetched clean towels from the linen cupboard near her bedroom and took him a sandwich at midday. Gramps liked his lunch at exactly twelve o'clock, and always had potted meat and brown bread with a buttered scone for afters. Mr Dutton always insisted that Abigail was exactly like Gramps!

After lunch the four friends met at the pond.

'What shall we do?' Nicola said. 'I'm riding at four o'clock so we've got three hours.'

'We could go to my house,' Katie-Marie suggested. 'I've got a video we could watch.'

'What video?' Claire said, suddenly interested.

'*Coppelia*, the full ballet! My dance teacher lent it to me, so that I can learn the Doll Dance.'

'I'm not watching that!' Claire said. 'Yuk!'

'Listen,' Abigail said quickly before there was an argument. 'Hill House is for sale!'

'So?' Nicola said, tossing her head. 'I know that already. My daddy's going to buy it and build thirty houses. I've seen the plans!'

'Why didn't you tell me?'

'Why should I, it's not your house! Just because you can see the trees from your window doesn't mean you own them! I can see the sweet shop from mine, but I don't get free Mars bars!'

Claire and Katie-Marie moved away, just a little, in case there was going to be trouble!

'But all the trees will be cut down. What about the squirrels, and the birds?' Abigail cried.

'They'll have to go and live somewhere else!'

'Don't you *care* Nicola? Trees are living things!'

'There's no For Sale notice,' Katie-Marie said, linking her arm in Abigail's to show her support. 'I can see the gates from our front room!'

'My daddy says they can't find somebody, a relative or something. He's been missing for ages. Missing people are presumed dead after seven years!' She said that with her nose in the air, sure that she knew something that the others didn't. 'After seven years it can be sold without permission . . . and that's in two months!'

'How do you know that?' Claire said.

'My daddy told me!'

Abigail didn't want to argue anymore.

'I just wish I could look inside, just once, before it goes.'

'Let's walk up Butler Lane. We might be able to squeeze through the gate or something,' Katie-Marie suggested.

'Claire couldn't squeeze through anything!' Nicola said, pinching the fleshy part of Claire's arm. Claire grinned. She didn't mind Nicola's teasing and opened a tube of Smarties with a flourish.

The girls walked up Butler Lane towards the back gate of Hill House. The high wall was covered in moss and creeping plants and the trees and bushes were growing right over it.

'Nobody could squeeze through that!' Claire said, making her fingers span the gaps in the wrought iron gate. 'Not even Katie-Marie, and she's skinny!'

'We could climb the wall?' Katie-Marie suggested.

'No we couldn't. My daddy wouldn't like it!'

'Your daddy hasn't bought it yet, so it doesn't belong to you either!' Claire argued. 'And I've seen boys climbing the walls to get conkers from the candle trees!'

'Candle trees? They're chestnut trees, stupid!' Nicola jeered.

'Well . . . they look as if they've got candles on them sometimes, and you can't eat the nuts so how can they be chestnuts?' Claire said.

'They're horse-chestnut trees, Claire. We eat sweet chestnuts. They're different,' Abigail said softly. 'And we mustn't go in, we'd be trespassing.'

'Somebody has been in, just look here!' Katie-Marie cried.

She was peering through the bars and the others bent close to see what she meant. There was a semi-circle of scraped earth and torn weeds, as though somebody had forced the gate over the tangled path.

'That's impossible!' Abigail whispered.

'Why? Somebody pushed hard, that's all!'

'But the gate opens from the other side!'

They all turned to look. The gate did open from the other side and the big padlock and chain were very rusty. Nobody had opened *that* for ages!

'How did they do it then?' Claire wondered.

Nicola put both hands at the top of the gate and leaned her weight against it. It opened, just a bit and only at the top. It would need a bit more effort to open it all.

'Look at this!' she cried. 'Somebody's taken the gate right off the hinges. It's only resting against the post!'

'Ouch!' Claire squealed as she tried to get through and scraped her knee on the wall.

'Shh! They could still be in there,' Abigail whispered.

'There's nobody in there!' Nicola said as she yanked the gate back into place. 'Daddy's been in, so he must have done it! If you're so bothered about the place, I'll ask him to let us look round before it's pulled down.'

'I think we should have gone in,' Claire said as they walked back down the lane.

'I don't,' Abigail said. 'It would be silly to go wandering about near an old building. We don't know if it's safe. Besides, you know we have to stay close to home. My dad would be really mad!'

'I suppose it will have to be the video then, there's nothing else to do!' Claire grumbled.

Claire and Nicola were kicking a pebble to each other, Katie-Marie was collecting pretty leaves and Abigail was deep in thought as the girl passed them. She smiled at Abigail and hurried on.

'I haven't seen *her* before!' Abigail said.

'Who?'

'The girl who just went past!'

'I didn't notice!'

The other three were still messing about when Abigail looked back. The girl wasn't there.

'She's gone in the gate!' she cried.

'Who?'

'That girl!'

'Rubbish!' Nicola said, kicking the pebble into the

road. 'She's gone to the houses up at the top!'

But there weren't any turnings on Butler Lane, not until it joined the main road and she hadn't had time to get *that* far!

Abigail didn't say any more but she still had a clear picture of the girl, in her head. She was small with very fair hair and her eyes were really big and blue and she was carrying a heavy shopping bag.

'You must have seen her,' she said as they crossed by the church. 'She was wearing a blue shell suit, nearly the same colour as my shirt!'

'I saw somebody,' Nicola said. 'But so what? People have a right to walk on the pavement, haven't they?'

But do they have a right to go into Hill House? Abigail thought, but she didn't say anything.

Chapter Four

Jilly pressed herself against the gate post and held her breath. Had the girl seen her squeeze through the gate?

She'd only managed to move it a little and had caught her ankle on the bottom rail. It was stinging and she was sure it was bleeding but she daren't move to look. What if the girl came back?

It was a long time before Jilly peeped out again. Butler Lane was empty and she sighed with relief. Her ankle *was* bleeding and it had run into her sock, but she hadn't been seen!

The walk through the grounds was lovely, now that Jilly had got used to the quiet. Being a town girl she hadn't met many squirrels and the only rabbits she knew belonged to Cathy. The rabbits who munched the grass of Hill House were quite unafraid of the human intruder. They looked at her, twitched their ears and went on eating. Cathy's rabbits had floppy ears that dangled in the sawdust and long silky fur. Jilly thought the wild rabbits were much nicer looking.

It made her sad, thinking of Cathy, and she didn't want Grandma to see an unhappy face, so she sat on an upturned plant pot until she felt better.

'Think happy thoughts!' she said aloud, and a bird answered, chirping away high up in one of the trees.

She couldn't spot him though.

'Where . . . are . . . you?' she sang.

The bird answered with a musical chirrup and they had a long conversation that made her smile again.

'Thank you, bird,' she said as she got up, picked up the shopping and started up the steps.

'You sound cheerful,' Grandma said.

'I was talking to a bird,' Jilly grinned.

'You'll be talking to the trees next!' Grandma said. 'Did you get everything?'

'Trees are living things too,' Jilly sighed. 'They whisper secrets to each other, just like gossips!'

Grandma shook her head as she unpacked the carrier bag.

'Wherever do you get your ideas from?' she said, 'Gossiping trees indeed!'

There had been a lot of improvements made in the week that the Potts had lived in the coach house. Grandad had found a bucket and a sweeping brush in his old garden shed that hadn't a roof any more, and Jilly had been down to the shops several times, for scrubbing brushes and cleaning things. The rooms over the garage were spotless, all of them, even though they were still camping out in one room. They used the kitchen, of course, and boiled a pan of water for washing themselves and the plastic plates and mugs. 'Potts washing pots?' Grandad always asked when Jilly and Grandma were washing up.

They had scrubbed the wooden floors and the tiles in the kitchen and bathroom, washed down the walls with something Grandma called 'sugar soap' and Grandad had repainted the iron table and chairs with half a tin of black he'd found in the garage.

There hadn't been much else down there. The one

with no door was full of rusty junk and logs and the end one had a padlock that Grandma's keys didn't fit.

'I bet there's *real* treasure in there!' Grandad said.

He'd made several trips to the shops at the bottom of Hill Top Road and those in Hillsby itself, coming back with second hand comforts: a hearth rug that wasn't very worn, another travel rug in tartan plaid, a cushion, a frying pan and a funny little cooking stove that burned methylated spirits.

'There's a bed going for fifteen pounds but I couldn't think how to get it here!' he said.

'We'll manage with the deck chairs,' Grandma said. 'I'm quite comfy.'

Jilly had gone with him to collect two little gas cylinders for the camping stove and it had been risky, both of them nipping through the gate.

Grandma unpacked the shopping, potatoes, beans, a tin of frankfurter sausages for tea and cornflakes and milk for morning.

'I wish we could have toast,' Jilly sighed. 'I really fancy some toast.'

'Never mind love. We'll pop out next week and find a cafe, then you can eat toast till it comes out of your ears!'

Jilly grinned. It was nice being with Grandma and Grandad, even if it was a bit scary, like today!

'Some girls were in the lane. I thought they'd seen me, but . . .'

'But?'

'But I don't think they saw me come in the gate. One of them looked really nice, and she smiled at me.'

Jilly thought about the girl while Grandma made tea, trying to picture her in her head.

'She was tall, much bigger than me, with curly black hair,' she muttered.

'Who?' Grandad asked, suddenly appearing in the kitchen doorway.

'A girl I saw in the lane. She was with some other girls but I don't think they saw me come in the gate.'

'What if they did? There were two lads half way over the wall last time I went out and there's a rope hanging from one of the elms so people do come into the grounds, young 'uns!'

'They might come near to the house, and see us!' Jilly cried.

'Why would they want to hang about these old garages? They're only after conkers! Stop worrying!'

But Jilly did worry, a lot.

'What if we never hear from Mum and Dad? What if we don't find out where they are? What if – '

'I'm going to change your name to What-if Potts if you don't stop that, Jilly!' Grandad said, a bit grumpily.

Jilly's eyes filled with tears. She hadn't meant to upset Grandad, he was probably just as worried as she was!

'I'm sorry, but I'm scared that I'll never see them again, and that they'll forget me!'

Grandma put both arms around Jilly and hugged the tears away.

'Listen, lovey. Grandad will go down to the phone box on Sunday morning and ring old Tom Bentley. He's been a good friend since our young days and your dad's got his number. He'll have told Tom what's happening and where we can contact him. It's all arranged, we just have to be patient.'

'Tomorrow?' Jilly asked, looking up at Grandma.

'Tomorrow!' Grandma nodded. 'And I know you're fed up with nothing to do all day so I'll show you Hill

House, shall I?'

Grandma took the keys from her bag and led Jilly across the cobbles, down the side of Hill House and round the back to the kitchen door.

Jilly was excited. The house was much bigger than she'd thought and as they went inside, into the dark, she felt a bit scared as well as excited. It had been empty for years and their footsteps echoed through the bare rooms.

The kitchen was big and quite modern with built-in pine units and two double sinks, but there were gaps where the cooker, fridge and dishwasher used to be. It was the same in the laundry. All the machines had gone, leaving taped-up wires and stopped-up pipes in the spaces where they'd been. It was sad.

When Grandma opened the door into the front hall Jilly couldn't stop the cry of astonishment that burst from her mouth.

'It's MEGA!'

'Thought you'd like it,' Grandma said.

'It's mega Grandma, huge!' Jilly said, less loudly.

The hall was a large semicircle with the front doors on the straight side. The windows were shuttered but there was light, coloured light, filtering through a round window high above the door and another on the first landing of an impressive flight of stairs that led to a balcony that curved to the right and left of them. The ceiling was so high that Jilly could hardly see it in the gloom.

'It goes right up to the roof!' she gasped, looking up.

'Nearly. There are two attics up above here and storage spaces in the roof over the bedrooms.'

Grandma pointed and Jilly could see the tops of the bedroom doors up on the two balconies.

It was lovely. The hall floor was made of marble slabs, black and white and arranged in a pattern that made a circle right under where the light should be.

'It was a chandelier, and it looked lovely, all lit up,' Grandma said, following Jilly's eyes up to the chain and cable that hung, abandoned, from the painted roof. 'And it was a two-day job to clean it!'

'Isn't it sad that no-one lives here any more?' Jilly said, still trying to make out what was painted on the hall ceiling.

'There aren't any Lyles left, at least I don't think there are. It's too big for people to manage, nowadays, and it would need a lot of work.'

Jilly had a tour of the ground floor, the rooms that led off the hall. All the doors were set between marble pillars with triangles at the top and the pillars were smooth and cold to touch. There was a morning room that caught the early sun, a dining room next to it and several smaller rooms behind the staircase that Grandma said were used as her pantry, sitting room and sewing room. The kitchens were at the back too and Jilly had already seen them.

On the West side of the hall was the lounge; a big room with a huge fireplace that burned logs, and alcoves that Grandma said had held marble statues of Greek goddesses; a study, lined with dusty bookshelves, and behind both rooms, with doors from each one, was a long conservatory with several broken panes of glass and a lot of dead plants.

'What a shame,' Grandma said, sadly. 'Mr Lyle loved his plants. There was a grapevine down that end and peaches all along the house wall. What a shame!'

As they went upstairs, Jilly noticed the cleaner squares of wallpaper where pictures had hung, big ones.

'This one here,' Grandma said, pointing to the empty space. 'This one here was a full length portrait of Mr Lyle's great, great grandfather . . . and this one was Giles Lyle, who fought at Waterloo!'

'Giles Lyle!' Jilly giggled. 'What a funny name!'

'Yes, and there was Nigel Lyle, Lionel Lyle and Miles Lyle, too, all the way up the stairs!'

Jilly had to sit on the stairs and hold her sides because she was laughing so much.

'What were the ladies called?' she spluttered.

'Good plain names like Mary and Martha! Mrs Lyle was Sarah, like me.'

'What about their children?'

'They never had any . . . never.'

Jilly had dirtied her clothes when she sat down on the grimy stairs.

'It all needs a good clean!' Grandma said, dusting off the dirty jeans with a rather heavy hand.

'Ouch! Let me do it!' Jilly cried.

After a tour of the bedrooms and two empty attics they went back downstairs, Jilly sliding down the banisters and adding another layer of dirt to her jeans.

'Why don't we?' she said as she dropped off at the bottom.

'What?'

'Give it a good clean? There's nothing else to do!'

'You've got books to read, Jilly,' Grandma said. 'You're missing school, remember?'

'I can do that at night. Why can't we, Grandma? Let's do it, let's make it shine again!'

Grandma looked at the house she had kept spotless for most of her life. It was sad to see it mildewed and dirty.

'It's a big job,' she said, thoughtfully.

'I'm a big girl!' Jilly grinned from her four feet four inches.

'You're a little girl with big ideas, lovey, but . . . if you want to, we'll have a go!'

As they were locking the kitchen door, Grandad passed carrying a cardboard box.

'Where are you off to?' Grandma asked. 'I've got plans that need you!'

'I reckon there's apples down by the back wall, and there's nobody but us, the worms, and a few lads scrumping to do 'em justice. Coming Jilly?'

She didn't need asking twice.

The grounds were really overgrown and it was hard to tell where the lawns had been. Grandad did a lot of sighing and tut-tutting as he held back the brambles for Jilly to get through difficult bits.

'It's like being in a jungle, isn't it Grandad?' she said. 'We're like explorers!'

'It's a crying shame, my word it is,' Grandad sighed. He'd kept the grounds so neat and now it was just an overgrown mess.

The paths were difficult to follow and they made a lot of detours before arriving at a small orchard with what had been the vegetable garden beyond it. The trees had been planted near the back wall and the vegetable garden and greenhouses were in the corner where the back wall met the one that ran along Butler Lane. Every pane of glass in the greenhouse was smashed, most of them by an enormous branch that had split and fallen from one of the tall trees.

'I had the finest tomatoes in the county in there,' Grandad muttered.

There were apples on the trees and a lot more rotting on the ground beneath.

'Now if we had an oven, and Grandma had a pie dish . . .'

'And a mixing bowl!' Jilly added.

'And a rolling pin!' Grandad said. 'We could have apple pie for tea! But as we haven't got any of those things, have an apple!'

Jilly munched away as they filled the box with apples, nice ones that hadn't got tiny holes to show that a creature was living inside.

'They're really juicy!' Jilly said, tossing her apple core onto the grass.

'Don't throw it there!' Grandad shouted, then he slapped his forehead. 'And why not?' he said, shaking his head.

Jilly grinned. The grass was squelchy with rotting apples and her core wouldn't make any difference to the mess.

'I'll have to get me a rake and clear this lot up, then you'll have to watch where you throw your rubbish, young lady!'

Grandad muttered all the way back through the grounds, about cutting this tree and pruning that and Jilly could see that *he* was going to be busy too!

Suddenly they came out of the trees into a paved clearing and there was the summer house.

'I do remember!' Jilly cried, hurrying across the moss-covered flags to peer inside.

Two of the panes of glass had gone and the rest were too dirty to see through. The wrought iron frame was rusty but the green copper cupola with its cockerel weather vane was still in place. Jilly climbed in over the low sill of the broken window. The floor was made of the same black and white marble blocks as the one in the house and she remembered playing hopscotch with a shoe-polish tin. It was a happy memory from when she was little, and Mum and Dad had brought her here to see Grandma and Grandad. It made her remember more about the place.

'There was a dog!' she said. 'A big red dog that I played with.'

'Mr Lyle's setter, Russet, that was. Fancy you remembering that!' Grandad said. 'Come on – Grandma will have tea ready.'

Jilly climbed out of the summer house and got to the edge of the paving before something made her turn and look up.

What was it?

The setting sun had caught the window of a house opposite, beyond the gardens and the road. Jilly couldn't see much of the house over the trees, just the chimneys and the gable window, lit by the sun.

She gulped, suddenly scared.

Could she be seen from that window?

Chapter Five

Abigail was still thinking about the fair-haired girl on Monday morning. She was sitting on the bench by the pond and staring at the ducks.

'Aren't you feeding them this morning?' Katie-Marie asked as she flopped onto the bench and dumped her school bag on the grass beside her.

'What?' Abigail jumped.

'The ducks! You're not feeding the ducks!'

'Yes I am,' Abigail mumbled, pulling the bread-bag out of her pocket and tipping out the crumbs in a small heap.

The ducks pounced on it and there was a great deal of noise as they squabbled and trod on each other's toes.

'Abby! You didn't share it!' Katie-Marie cried. 'Are you sick or something?'

'No, I . . . I was thinking!'

'What about?' Katie-Marie said, getting to her feet and swinging her bag over her shoulder.

'That girl we saw in Butler Lane,' Abigail muttered, still thinking as she set off across the grass, without even saying goodbye to the ducks.

'The one *you* saw, Abby. I didn't really notice her,' Katie-Marie said as she followed Abigail down the road.

'You're late!' Nicola shouted as they neared her house. 'You know I don't like to be late!'

'It was Abigail, she was thinking!' Katie-Marie said, adding, 'about that girl!' in a teasing voice.

Nicola rolled her eyes and pulled a face.

'It was only a girl from the estate at the top of the lane!' she sighed. 'What's so special about that?'

'I think I saw her in Hill House gardens on Saturday. It was tea-time and I was just upstairs getting – '

'We don't want to know what you were doing! Just tell us what you saw, Abby!' Nicola snapped impatiently.

'I saw somebody with blonde hair among the bushes near the summer house!'

'I bet it was a cat! There's a mushroom coloured one living next door to me,' Katie-Marie suggested.

'Who cares,' Nicola complained. 'I've got more to think about than moggies with mushroom fur! Look at Claire!'

Claire was waiting by the school gates and she was hugging a large oblong box.

'What's that?' Nicola asked, poking the box.

'My keyboard! It's projects today, isn't it? I'm going to write a song about clowns then sing it onto a tape. It could be a HIT!'

'We're supposed to be doing a history, not writing songs!' Nicola insisted. 'You never listen, Claire!'

Abigail sighed. Nicola was always bossy!

'We can do anything we like as long as it's about entertainment,' she said. 'I'm going to do a project on the Elizabethan theatre, I've got a book about it.'

'You've got a book about *everything* at your house, it's like a library!' Nicola said, tossing her head as she went through the school gates.

Abigail didn't say anything. It would only make Nicola think of another comment. She always liked to have the last word.

She was glad when the bell went and Katie-Marie slipped an arm through hers as they walked into school.

'She's just being Nicola, Abby. Don't mind her,' she whispered.

The morning seemed to drag on and on and Claire couldn't concentrate because her keyboard was in the store cupboard and she couldn't wait to play it. She tapped her finger nails on her desk lid, tapped her teeth with her pencil and shuffled her feet so much that her desk shook, as well as Nicola's who was next to her.

'Sit still, Claire,' she warned. 'Or I'll tell!'

At last it was lunch-time and when that was over everybody went in for the register with big smiles on their faces.

'Can I get my keyboard out now, please, Miss Newton?' Claire cried excitedly, her hand already on the handle of the storeroom door.

'Just wait until we get organised, Claire,' Miss Newton said kindly. 'There's a lot to do!'

Most of the class stayed in the room and all the art materials were put out on the long table at the back. On Miss Newton's desk were all the books about entertainment that she could find and Nicola was first there to get the book about horses. She had decided to do a project about 'Horses on Show' and had a lot of ideas.

Martin, who was going to learn to juggle for his 'Jester' project, was sent to the hall with Claire and her keyboard and Katie-Marie with her tapes and tape recorder, Claire's keyboard had earphones so that she could compose her tunes while Katie-Marie played her ballet music.

Mr Johnson was going to be in the hall to keep an eye on them and see that they didn't hurt themselves – or the hall!

'I can do my work here as well as in my office, and I like to know what's going on!' he said, wagging his finger at Martin.

Abigail was thrilled! Miss Newton had arranged something special for her, an afternoon in the library with all its reference books.

'You're expected, Abigail, and Mr Porter will be glad to help your research. You can go straight home from there at the end of the afternoon,' Miss Newton said as she saw Abigail across the road. Abigail was used to crossing the road by herself, every morning, but Miss Newton explained that *she* was responsible for her until four o'clock and had to be sure she was safe.

Nicola was sulking when she left, and muttering about people being favourites, but Abigail decided to smile and say nothing. It was too nice an afternoon for quarrels, and by home-time Nicola would be out of her mood and they could all walk home together, as always.

The library was empty except for Mr Porter and the Junior Librarian, who was sticking new date sheets in a pile of books.

'Well here you are, Miss Dutton. Everything's ready for you!' Mr Porter said, with a smile.

Mr Porter had been at the library a long time, as long as Abigail had been a member and a long time before that. Mr Dutton said that Mr Porter had looked *exactly* the same when *he* was a boy and even Gramps had known him for ages.

Mr Porter was very tall and thin. He had grey hair, grey eyes and silver-rimmed glasses with lilac-tinted lenses. He always wore a grey suit, a silvery tie with black stripes and grey socks which showed where his too short trousers left a gap between them and his shiny black shoes. Abigail supposed that he couldn't get trousers to fit his long legs, and always tried hard to be serious when she talked to him because he always made her want to giggle. He was just like the meerkats she had seen on a TV programme He held his hands in front of him, just like they did, and his pointed face darted this way and that to supervise the whole library. He always looked as if he was seeing and listening to something that no-one else could see and hear.

'Now then,' Mr Porter said. 'If you'll just follow me to the reference section, I've put a few interesting books out for you. Have you got a pencil?'

'Yes Mr Porter, thank you,' Abigail said politely.

There were several books on the table and Abigail soon forgot the library and Mr Porter as she dipped into this book, then that and filled three pages of her notebook with neat writing.

About half way through the afternoon, Mr Porter appeared at her table.

'You are working hard!' he said. 'Here's something you might be interested in.'

It was a book about the local area and there was a whole chapter on Hill Top. Abigail already knew that it had once been a village, a small one, before the nearby town had grown and it had become just a suburb. There was a map showing the village as it had been before the old cottages had been pulled down to make room for the terraces that Katie-Marie lived in, and there was a forest where Nicola's house and her dad's builders' yard was now.

Abigail sighed. She would have liked Hill Top when it was just a village.

Over the page was a pen and ink drawing of St Luke's, which was fifteenth century, and another labelled 'Hill House, an impression from a painting by William Glade'.

Abigail forgot about Shakespeare and The Globe theatre as she read about Hill House. The paragraph had caught her eye because the house didn't look at all like the one she knew – this Hill House had two wings and a middle bit that made it E shaped, and was built of wood and plaster. It was all black and white, like Little Moreton Hall, in Cheshire, where she'd been on holiday.

'A fine example of Elizabethan architecture, destroyed by fire in 1803' the caption read.

Abigail read further to discover that the Lyle family had rebuilt the house in the Georgian style, with sash windows each with twelve panes. Georgian architecture was all pillars and straight lines and it was the Victorian architects who had added the bay windows, the turret rooms, the conservatory, and the summer house.

Abigail drew a picture of the black and white house and read everything else she could find about Hill Top and the Lyle family who had lived at Hill House and owned all the land around it.

'It's all very sad!' she said to Mr Porter as he helped her to put the books back in their places. 'All people want to do is pull down lovely old places and put red-brick boxes on the land. There won't be anything beautiful left to look at by the time I'm grown up!'

'Oh, you'll grow up and move on, Abigail. Everybody does! I grew up among the chimneys and fires of Sheffield's steel works and I thought it was wonderful. I loved the black streets and the noise. I never thought I'd settle anywhere else, but I did. You'll find another place and be happy in it . . . everything changes,' Mr Porter sighed.

'I won't!' Abigail said as she left the library to wait for her friends. 'I won't leave Hill Top, ever!'

As soon as the others came out of school and crossed the zebra to join her, Abigail started to tell them about Hill House.

'Did you know there was another house, before the one that's there now?'

'What?' Nicola said, staring at her.

'Another house, another Hill House, an Elizabethan one!'

'So?' Nicola said. 'If it isn't there now it isn't important!'

'That's the same as saying that because William Shakespeare's dead, he isn't important!' Abigail argued.

'Well he isn't! He makes no difference to me!' Nicola snapped, linking arms with Claire. 'Are you coming to my house for a bit, Clara-Cluck? I've got a new computer game.'

Nicola and Claire walked in front as the four girls strolled up Hill Top Road. Now and then Claire would look back and grin, then say something to Nicola and they both laughed.

'I don't know why we're friends with Nicola!' Katie-Marie grumbled. 'She's always bossy and says nasty things!'

'She's just being Nicola, she doesn't mean it,' Abigail sighed.

'You're too nice!' Katie-Marie said. 'Ooops! I forgot to go to the shops! Are you coming back with me?'

'I'd better go straight home,' Abigail said.

'See you in the morning, then,' Katie-Marie promised, as she turned back towards the roundabout and the zebra crossings.

Abigail walked up the road behind Nicola and Claire, who turned and waved as they went into Nicola's smart new house. She smiled and waved back.

'I don't like computer games anyway,' she said to a duck who had strayed onto the pavement. 'Shoo, get back to the pond where you're safe!'

Abigail was so intent on getting the duck home that she didn't notice the girl until her head was bobbing above the wall where the stream ran under the road.

It was her!

Abigail forgot about being home on time and hurried after the small figure with its shopping bag, taking care as she crossed the road.

'This time I'll see where she goes,' she muttered.

She waited on the corner, hidden by the big gatepost and watched the mystery girl as she hurried to the back gate, looked back once then slipped in.

'I knew it!' Abigail said, running as fast as she could to slip through the hinged side of the gate only moments after the other girl. She could see the track and followed it, catching up with the girl by an archway of trees.

'Wait!' she called.

The girl stopped, dropping the carrier bag and spilling tins and packets all over the grass and dead leaves.

'Oh no!' she cried, scrambling to catch a bean can before it rolled under a bramble.

'I'm sorry, I didn't mean to scare you,' Abigail said.

'Well you did!' the girl wailed, almost in tears.

'Who are you! What are you doing here? I saw you last week didn't I? I knew I wasn't seeing things and you were near the summer house on Saturday, at tea-time!' Abigail said, talking so fast that she didn't stop for a breath.

'Don't tell, oh please don't tell!' the girl said, starting to cry properly.

'Tell what? I don't understand, who are you?'

'Jilly. I'm Jilly Potts,' she said, drying her eyes on the bottom of her T-shirt. 'And I've got to take the shopping in. If you wait here, I'll come back and explain.'

'Promise?' Abigail asked.

'Promise!' Jilly nodded. She'd liked the tall girl that first time they'd met, in the lane. She had a friendly smile. 'I won't be a minute, then I'll tell you,' she said, hurrying through the bushes towards the house.

Abigail leaned on one of the trees, looking up through the autumn leaves to the blue sky above. At last she was in the grounds of Hill House and it was just as she'd imagined. It was another world, full of green and gold with splashes of purple and red. She could hear birds, creatures rustling the undergrowth and the Zzzzz and Mmmmm of tiny insects. A millipede ran right over her brown school shoe and a red and black butterfly had settled on her green school bag.

'At last!' she sighed.

'I wasn't *that* long!' Jilly said, appearing from a tangle of rhododendron and bramble.

'I meant at last I'm here, in Hill House!' Abigail explained.

Jilly led her through the gardens to the summer house and they climbed in through the broken window. It was cool and quiet and Jilly had found a board and two plant pots to make a bench. She felt comfortable with Abigail, as though they had been friends for years.

'Can I trust you?' she asked.

'Of course you can!' Abigail nodded.

*

It was later, when Abigail was walking home that she thought about her promise. She could almost hear Dad's voice telling her that it isn't a kindness to keep a secret, if it allows someone to break the law. She had promised not to tell, but Mr and Mrs Potts *were* trespassing, and Jilly *was* playing truant and living without even a proper bed in a bare room with candles!

Abigail didn't know what to do.

'You're very late!' Mrs Dutton said as Abigail went in by the kitchen door. 'Where have you been until now?'

'I've been in the library all afternoon and went on working after school was over, then I went to Nicola's to see her new game,' she said, quietly. 'I didn't realise how late it was, I'm sorry.'

It was awful! Now she had told a lie!

'And look at the state of your clothes!' Mrs Dutton went on. 'You look as though you've been pulled through a hedge backwards!'

Abigail gulped. She couldn't say it was true, or that she'd been through more than one! Oh dear, she did hate to be deceitful!

As she went upstairs to change her clothes, Daniel popped his head out of the boys' bedroom.

'Abby! Come and look at my painting!' he cried.

'I've got more important things to do than look at your blotchy messes!' she snapped.

Daniel's happy face changed to a sad one and his door closed quietly.

Things were going from bad to worse!

After she had changed into comfortable clothes, Abigail stood at her bedroom window, took a long look at Hill House, then closed her eyes. There was always someone she could talk to.

'I need help, Jesus,' she said softly. 'I've promised to keep a secret when I know it's wrong, I've told a lie to my mum and I've just upset my little brother. What do I do now?'

Chapter Six

Jilly woke with her heart thumping and sat up, almost tipping her sun-lounger bed.

For a few moments she couldn't remember where she was and looked to right and left, very frightened, until two familiar lumps that were Grandma and Grandad stirred under their travel rugs and Grandma coughed.

Her heart stopped pounding as the bare little room became familiar and she knew where she was.

'What's to do?' Grandad grunted as he heaved himself out of the low deck chair. 'You're awake early!'

'I had a bad dream, Grandad, but I can't remember what it was about,' Jilly said, still a bit scared.

'That's the last time you have a late supper then! Supper always makes *me* dream!'

Grandma had heated a tin of tomato soup just before Jilly had got into bed. It had started to rain and the evening had been a cold one, the first after the long hot summer. It had been cosy, sipping hot soup while the rain beat on the windowpanes.

The dream forgotten, Jilly jumped out of bed and went into the bathroom to get washed. Grandma was still in her chair and Grandad was lighting the little cooker when they heard Jilly's cry.

'There's water everywhere!'

The rain was pouring in through a crack in the ceiling and falling right where a person would stand to get washed.

'You'll have to use the kitchen sink, Jilly!' Grandad said. 'It's raining more in here than it is outside!'

Jilly turned the tap on and it was really cold.

'I wish we could have *hot* water,' she sighed.

'You can have what's left after I've made a cup of tea, if you want,' Grandma said, as she found another cardigan to put on top of the one she was wearing. 'It's a bit chilly this morning. Let's have the stove on, Grandad.'

Jilly didn't wait for the hot water after all. The cold wash woke her up quickly and she helped to get breakfast ready while Grandad had a look in the loft.

'It's a slate or two that's gone, by the look of it, but I'll have to fix it from inside because I'm not going on the roof' he said as he appeared in the doorway, rubbing his hands at the sight of baked beans and fried egg. 'I'll go and call Tom Bentley, this morning, there might be a message from your dad, Jilly!'

'And we're going to do a bit of cleaning in the big house, aren't we love?' Grandma said, smiling at Jilly as she put a plastic plate in front of her.

Jilly ate her beans and wondered what to do. Should she tell Grandma and Grandad about Abigail Dutton? They had met every day, just for a few minutes and yesterday, being Friday, Abigail had managed a whole hour while Mrs Dutton shopped at the supermarket and Mr Dutton took Daniel and Matthew for their swimming lesson. They'd arranged to meet in the summer house on Sunday afternoon. What if somebody saw her?

'I saw that girl again, yesterday. The one I thought

had seen me come in the gate,' Jilly said as she helped to clear the table.

'Well I hope she didn't see you this time! I don't want to spend my old age in prison!'

Jilly knew that Grandad was joking. She could see the twinkle in his eye and the way he winked at Grandma when he thought Jilly wasn't looking.

'No, she didn't see me!' she said, hoping she was right about trusting her new friend.

'Let's start in here,' Grandma said as they entered the hall from the kitchen door.

Grandad had found an old mop head in the garage and had fixed it onto a stout branch that had fallen from one of the trees. Grandma had boiled the mop in an old bucket, to get it clean and to stop it from smelling. They had a proper sweeping brush, a scrubbing brush, two pieces of old towelling, an old shirt for a duster and a bucket of hot water.

Jilly started to sweep while Grandma set to work on the staircase. The black and white tiles were dirty and covered in leaves that had blown in through a broken window with loose shutters. Jilly opened the shutters to see better and just as she did it, the sun broke through the clouds and sent a dusty shaft of light onto the fancy circle of tiles. It brought the old house to life.

'I don't know why we're doing this!' Grandma grunted as she poked a cloth between the carved banister posts. 'I don't suppose anybody will see it!'

'Not if it's going to be knocked down!' Jilly said.

She could have bitten off her tongue as soon as she'd said it!

'What do you mean, knocked down?'

Jilly gulped and tried to think fast.

'I – I thought,' she stammered, 'I thought old buildings were always knocked down, if nobody wants them.'

'Of course they're not, silly! People don't knock things down just because they're old. What about me and Grandad?'

Jilly grinned. She could just imagine somebody trying to knock Grandad down! She did feel uncomfortable, keeping her friendship with Abigail a secret, but was sure she wouldn't tell anybody that the Potts were living at Hill House.

They worked all morning, sweeping out the elegant dining room and study and cleaning the dust and grime from the bookshelves and mouldings, only breaking off for lunch at one o'clock.

Grandad thought he had fixed the hole in the roof but it had stopped raining so he couldn't really tell.

'I'm going down the garden to look at my greenhouses,' he said. 'There's another shed down there and if there's a rake or a broom left behind, I'll do a bit of cleaning up.'

'I thought you were going to – ' Jilly began.

'Done it! And it's good news. I went down to the phone box first thing, and Tom's heard from your dad. He's left a number and you can ring him yourself.'

'Now?' Jilly cried, her face lighting up with a huge grin.

'Not now, they'll be moving their things!'

'Where, Grandad? Where are they?'

'They'll be starting work on Monday, in the kitchen of a big hotel in London, and they've got rooms there. They'll be waiting for your call at twelve o'clock tomorrow!'

There were almost two whole days to wait, but it was good news and Jilly set to work on the drawing room with a happy face. Things were working out, Mum and Dad had a place to stay and she was safe with Grandma and Grandad, as long as Abigail kept the secret.

Jilly swept the floor and cleaned the dead leaves from the fireplace. She thought it was strange that they had managed to fall down the chimney, until she stood in the grate and looked up. It was a big fireplace and there was plenty of room to stand, if she bent her knees a bit. The chimney was *huge*! It was square and she could see right up to the sky. The brick walls were blackened from years of smokey fires and here and there was a brick that jutted out, making a little ledge or foothold.

Jilly shuddered, remembering a history lesson at school. This was just the sort of chimney that a boy would climb, to sweep the soot down with a little brush.

Grandma was somewhere out in the hall when Jilly heard the noise. She had been cleaning the door posts with a damp cloth and everything was quiet and peaceful. She was working out a story in her head, a story about meeting her mum and dad in London and all living together again in a nice house. She imagined what Dad would say and what Mum would do and how happy everybody would be.

The noise came from somewhere near the window and Jilly's heart missed a beat. She froze, her hand on the door knob and her eyes on the window.

When it happened again she didn't wait to find out what it was, but flung open the door and bumped into Grandma. Over went the bucket and the dirty water swirled all over the marble tiles.

'Whatever are you playing at, Jilly?' Grandma began. She was quite cross until she saw Jilly's scared face. 'What is it? What's the matter? Have you hurt yourself?'

Jilly shook her head and tried to speak.

'There's – there's something in there!' she squeaked, pointing towards the drawing room.

'Whatever could be in there, Jilly? The place has been locked up for years,' Grandma said, heading for the door.

'Don't go in, Grandma!' Jilly cried. 'It will *get* you!'

Grandma laughed then stood with her hands on her hips.

'Well! Where is it?' she said.

Jilly peered into the room. There wasn't anything in there, and she was beginning to feel a bit stupid when it happened again; a sort of scratchy, scuffling sound from somewhere over by the window.

'Now I did hear that, myself!' Grandma said. 'There's something in the window seat. A mouse, that's what it is!'

Jilly sighed with relief. She wasn't afraid of mice. Grandma went across to the window seat and tapped on it, but there weren't any more noises.

'It won't lift up,' she said, trying to open it.

Jilly tried at the other end but the lid of the window seat was nailed down.

'Go and find Grandad and tell him to come, and bring his claw hammer with him!'

Jilly went out into the sunshine. It was lovely and warm after the coolness of the house. The rain had left everything dripping wet. There was a smell of moist earth and wet grass and every leaf had its own diamond raindrop earring, dangling from its tip.

Grandad was in the first greenhouse, sorting plant pots into sizes and clearing the dead plants from them.

'Well, Jilly! Have you finished cleaning the place already?' he asked.

Jilly shook her head.

'Grandma wants you to come and bring your claw hammer. There's something in the window seat and the lid's nailed down.'

'How do you know there's something in there if you can't open the lid?' Grandad said as he wiped his hands on an old duster.

'We heard it!' Jilly explained.

'It'll be mice. Get everywhere, they do!'

Grandad hurried to the coach house to get the big hammer he had found in the garage.

'I had a feeling I'd need this, sooner or later,' he said.

It took a while to get the lid open. There were nails all around it and the tops had been filed off so that they didn't show. There weren't any more noises but when they did get the lid open a cloud of paper, shredded into tiny pieces, rose up like dust.

'It's mice, all right! They've been chewing these old newspapers to make their nest!' Grandad said, poking about with his hammer. 'What's this?'

The hammer had hit something hard and when Grandad pulled it out it was a package, wrapped in thick brown paper and tied with string. It had been wrapped in newspaper too, but that was shredded and almost gone.

'Look at these tiny teeth marks,' Jilly cried, holding up a large corner of newsprint.

'Mice!' Grandad grunted, lifting another parcel out of the seat. 'This one's heavy!'

Right at the bottom was a book – an old ledger – and Grandma decided it was time to stop.

'The light's going and it's time we had some tea,' she said.

'Right! We'll take this lot back and see what's in the

parcels. They're heavy!' Grandad said.

There were five altogether, and when the newspaper had been removed, the brown packages were labelled '32', '6', '14', '23' and '9'.

'What does it mean? What are the numbers for?' Jilly asked.

Grandad opened the ledger. There were a few pages full of curvy writing, then a numbered list. Several of the numbered entries were ticked, and Grandad got very excited.

'What is it? What's to do?' Grandma said.

'It's an inventory!' Grandad said. 'A list of items. Open that one labelled 9.'

Grandma cut the string and peeled the brown paper from the object. It was a plate, and it was very heavy.

'That's right!' Grandad cried. 'Now open all the others!'

There was a large goblet with four red stones set round it, an embroidered cloth, a pair of candlesticks and a cross. They were very beautiful.

Jilly's mouth was wide open and Grandma had forgotten all about food.

'It's treasure!' she said.

'It's some of the family's heirlooms,' Grandad said. 'Look! It says here that they were found when digging the foundations for an extension. That'll be the conservatory, I'll bet. And here, in the ledger, are ticks against the things we've found. There's a lot more stuff listed though!'

'Does that mean there's more to find? Shall we go and look?' Jilly said excitedly.

'It means a lot more than that, Jilly. This changes things a bit. We can't keep this stuff. It'll have to be handed in, to the estate. It must have been Mr Lyle's father, or grandfather that dug these up and hid them in the window seat. What's the date on that newspaper?'

Jilly sifted through the yellow, fragile bits until she found the top half of the page.

'May 6th, 1863,' she read. 'It's over a hundred years old, this paper!' she said, holding it very carefully.

'Monday morning, first thing, we'll take them down to Mr Forbes. He was the Lyle's solicitor. He'll know what to do,' Grandad said.

'But they'll know we've been living here, Grandad, and we might go to prison!' Jilly said.

'We will if we keep these, Jilly,' Grandad said, shaking his head. 'They're pure gold!'

Chapter Seven

Abigail woke up with a headache on Sunday morning and didn't feel like breakfast at all. Saturday had been a long day. It was quite a journey to Aunty Carol's house and the bus had stopped and started and swayed from side to side all the way there. It was smelly too, the hot engine fumes making her feel sick and impatient with Daniel who had bounced up and down on the seat beside her, telling her to look at sheep, cows, a dead tree, two birds and anything else that caught his eye.

'The baby's gorgeous, but I hate the bus ride!' she groaned as she got dressed.

Daniel was tucking into his cornflakes. Bus rides never bothered him and he greeted Abigail with a big smile.

'I'm going to paint a picture of baby June, Abby!' he shouted, splattering cornflakes everywhere.

'Please don't shout, Daniel,' Abigail moaned, holding her head.

'Don't you feel well?' Mrs Dutton asked, passing her a small glass of orange juice. 'I know the bus upsets your tummy!'

'It doesn't upset mine!' Daniel said, shouting again and starting on his scrambled eggs on toast.

'That's because it's made of cast iron!' Mrs Dutton

said. 'Be quiet and eat, Daniel! Perhaps you'd better give church a miss this morning,' she went on, feeling Abigail's forehead.

'No! I'm fine. I want to go to church, really. I'll be all right when I've had some toast!'

'Is there something bothering you, Abby?' Mrs Dutton asked, when the boys had gone upstairs to get ready. 'Is there something wrong at school or have you fallen out with Nicola again?'

Abigail really wanted to talk to her mum, to tell her about Hill House, and the Potts, but she couldn't break her promise to Jilly.

'There's nothing wrong, it's just the bus ride, that's all,' she said quietly.

It was peaceful in church. The Duttons sat right at the front in the family pew and even Daniel sat still and listened while the organ played as people came in. Mrs Dutton and her ladies' circle had decorated the chancel with white chrysanthemums and sprays of copper beech and they looked lovely against the polished wood of the pulpit and choir stalls.

When Mr Dutton came in everybody stood up and sang the first hymn, 'Blessed be the tie that binds', then knelt for a few moments of silent prayer. Abigail asked for good health and happiness for her family, that Jilly and her family would find an answer to their problems, and for guidance in deciding what to do.

When Mr Dutton read the lesson it did seem as if the last part of her prayer had been answered. Abigail listened carefully.

'*When the Son of Man comes as King, and all the angels with him, he will sit on his royal throne and all the earth's people will be gathered before him. Then he will divide them into two groups, just as a shepherd separates the sheep from the goats; he will put the sheep at his right and the goats at his left. Then the King will say to the people on his right, "You who are blessed by my Father; Come! Come and receive the Kingdom which has been prepared for you ever since the creation of the world. I was hungry and you fed me, thirsty and you gave me drink; I was a stranger and you received me in your homes, naked and you clothed me; I was sick and you took care of me. In prison and you visited me." The righteous will then answer him: "When, Lord, did we ever see you hungry and feed you, or thirsty and give you drink? When did we ever see you a stranger and welcome you in our homes, or naked and clothe you? When did we ever see you sick or in prison, and visit you?" The King will answer back, "I tell you indeed, whenever you did this for one of the least important of these brothers of mine, you did it for me!"* Matthew 25, verses 31 to 41.'

Mr Dutton paused, giving the congregation time to think, then he went on –

'Next Sunday we shall celebrate the good things that God gives us each day, each month and each year. Every autumn we bring the bounty of the earth to the altar, in thanks for another year of rich harvests and personal gifts of health and prosperity, but this year I am asking for a different harvest, a harvest of money to buy hope, shelter and comfort for those in need.

'Jesus said, when you do it for the needy you do it for him. When Mother Teresa of Calcutta was asked how she could touch the leper and bathe his wounds, she answered that every time she touched the leper's sores she touched the Lord.

'We all support and help our families and our good neighbours but this year I am asking you to think of those who are less likeable, those whose lifestyles we fear and would not welcome in our homes and those who have fallen victim to the pressures of our society. They are all part of the shepherd's flock, and lost.

'I am asking you to give, all you can, to support those struggling with addictions, alcohol and drugs; for those caught in the poverty trap who turn to crime in their despair, for mothers and children in safe havens, fleeing from violent homes; for those in prisons and for the homeless in desperate need, for when you do a kindness for one of these, our brothers, you do it for him.

'There will be a tree with bare branches in church next Sunday. I am asking you to bring your gifts in envelopes and hang them on the branches to bring our money-tree to life, so that it can enrich the lives of those in need.'

The congregation sang 'When I needed a neighbour' and Abigail felt better, just a little bit. The Potts were homeless and she was helping them by not telling anybody they were there. She wouldn't even have known they were there if she hadn't followed Jilly that day. She was being a good neighbour, a sheep not a goat!

But that doesn't mean it's all right to tell lies! she thought. That part did bother her and she wished Jilly hadn't made her promise.

At lunch-time the family sat at the dining room table and Mrs Dutton put the roast and vegetables in the heated trolley for Abigail to take through from the kitchen. It was roast lamb and the smell of the mint sauce on the table was making Abigail's mouth water. She couldn't help feeling sad for Jilly, managing with a tiny picnic stove and a pan. Jilly wouldn't be having Sunday dinner!

Mr Dutton said grace then started to carve the meat.

'Isn't there a story about some children being asked to give their dinner to a poor neighbour?' he asked.

'*Little Women*,' Abigail said, passing her plate. 'Meg, Jo, Amy and Beth take their Christmas breakfast to a poor lady who's just had a baby.'

'We're not taking our dinner to Aunty Carol are we?' Daniel cried, his eyes and mouth open in horror. 'I'll put all my pennies in my envelope!'

'Nobody's going to take your dinner, Daniel. Sit still and pass your plate!' Mrs Dutton laughed.

'It's sad that people have nowhere to live, isn't it?' Abigail said as she looked at the polished table, the cork mats, the silver knives and forks and the blue willow-pattern plates. 'We're very lucky!'

'Andrew Norris has got a swimming pool at his house. He's lucky!' Matthew said.

'It's not luck that gets swimming pools, Matthew. It's doing well at school, getting a good job and working hard!' Mrs Dutton said.

'Dad works hard and we haven't got one, or a new car . . . that goes!' Matthew grumbled.

'Or new bikes!' Daniel added, his mouth full of meat even before he'd been served with potatoes.

'My rewards are different,' Mr Dutton said with a smile.

Abigail tried to bring the conversation back to the homeless.

'But it's a shame people have got nowhere to live when there are empty houses all over the place. There's two down Hill Road and there's Hill House!'

'Empty houses belong to somebody, Abigail. I'm

afraid it's up to them whether they let people live in them or not,' Mr Dutton said.

'What would happen if somebody did get into an empty house, and live in it?'

'They'd be squatters and could be evicted by the police, and prosecuted. There's a law against trespassing.'

'How can they live in an empty house, there wouldn't be any furniture, or lights!' Matthew said.

'Or dinner!' Daniel cried, and everybody laughed. Daniel did like his food!

After lunch there was a knock at the front door. It was Katie-Marie and her stepfather.

'We're going to a children's farm, Abby. Do you want to come?' Katie-Marie asked.

'That'll be nice, Abigail. You go and have a good time,' Mrs Dutton said from the kitchen doorway.

'I'm not feeling too good. I don't fancy a car ride after yesterday,' Abigail said.

Katie-Marie looked sad then cross and went down the path without looking back.

'I wish they'd asked me!' Matthew said.

'Well they didn't!' Abigail snapped and her face went red when she caught her mother's eye.

'I don't think I know you at the moment, Abby. There was no need for that. It would have been nice for Matthew.'

'Katie-Marie's my friend, not his,' Abigail said, trying to make things right.

'She won't be your friend much longer if your temper gets any worse. I don't know what's got into you!'

Abigail did! It was all the worry. She mumbled something about her head hurting and ran up to her room. How could she go with Katie-Marie when Jilly would be waiting for her, and how could she explain that to her mum?

'It would have been nice though,' she sighed as she looked out of her window and saw what a lovely day it was.

At two o'clock, she changed into jeans and sweatshirt and said she felt like a walk in the fresh air.

'Can I come?' Daniel asked.

'I just want to be by myself, till this headache's gone, Danny,' she sighed.

That was another lie, the headache had gone!

She went out by the kitchen door, through the back garden, across the churchyard with its ancient gravestones and through the wishing gate to the common land and the pond. That way no-one would suspect she was going up Butler Lane.

'Hi, Abracadabra!'

It was Nicola, running across the grass to join her.

'Don't call me that, Nicola, it's stupid!'

'Pardon me for talking!' Nicola said, tossing her head. 'What's the matter with you?'

'Nothing. I just want to be by myself'

'Why can't we be by ourselves together? Claire's gone out with her mum and Katie-Marie's not in.'

'She's gone to a children's farm. She called for me but I don't want to go,' Abigail said, not meaning to upset Nicola.

'Oh great!' she complained. 'Nobody bothers to ask me if I want to go! Some friends you lot are!'

'I really don't want to do anything, Nicola. I'm going home,' Abigail said. 'See you.'

And that's lie number six, she thought as she left Nicola standing by the pond. She went round the church as if she was going home that way and Nicola was nowhere in sight when she looked back.

'Thank goodness,' she sighed, then darted across the road and up Butler Lane.

Jilly was waiting in the summer house with a Kit Kat, a can of Coke and two plastic mugs.

'A picnic!' she grinned, sharing the Coke into the mugs.

'I do like this place,' Abigail said, watching a thrush pecking at something between the paving stones outside.

'So do I, and I've got a lot to tell you!' Jilly said.

Abigail was really excited when she heard about the treasure.

'What are you going to do with it?' she asked. 'It must be worth a lot of money!'

'Grandad's taking it to Mr Lyle's solicitor, tomorrow.'

'But you'll be found out, he'll know you're trespassing!' Abigail gasped.

Jilly shrugged her shoulders.

'Grandad says there's nothing else we can do, even though we'll have to move again, and I don't know where! I'm just getting used to it too!'

'Do you really *have* to tell?' Abigail asked sadly.

'Yes, and I hope we don't get put in prison! Grandad says there could be a lot more treasure, hidden and buried, so we can't just forget it, can we? At least you'll only have to keep our secret another day!' Jilly said.

'I wish we could go and look in the house, before you leave it and it's pulled down,' Abigail sighed.

Jilly delved into the back pocket of her jeans and held up a large key.

'We can,' she said. 'Grandad's gone to a car boot sale in Ridley and Grandma's asleep, so I've borrowed the key!'

Abigail could hardly breathe as Jilly unlocked the kitchen door of Hill House, her house, the one she had dreamed of seeing some day.

'I knew it would look like this!' she whispered, gazing at the wide staircase and the black and white floor. 'It's so clean!'

'It should be, we've worked hard, me and Grandma!'

'Did you know it's built on top of another house, an Elizabethan one? It burned down in 1803!'

Abigail told Jilly all the things she had found out about the Lyles and Hill House and Jilly took her on a tour, all the way up to the attics.

'This is where we found the things,' she said, lifting the lid of the window seat in the drawing room. It was empty but for the bits of paper the mice had left. 'Somebody must have dug them up, put them in here and forgotten them.'

'How could anybody forget they'd done that?' Abigail wondered.

'Perhaps they died without telling anybody . . . and look, the nails hardly show, so you wouldn't know there was a space under there!'

'Is there a space in the other front room?'

'No, we've looked. It's just a windowsill, a wide one,' Jilly said.

'Perhaps there's a secret room, or a passage?' Abigail suggested.

They were tapping the panelling in the study when they heard Jilly's Grandma calling.

'Jilly! Are you in here, Jilly?'

They held their breath while Jilly peeped through the crack of the door and waited until Grandma went into the dining room.

'Quick!' she mimed, creeping out across the hall and

through the door by the stairs. 'Keep to the bushes and watch out for Grandad coming back.'

'When will I see you?' Abigail whispered.

'Tomorrow, after school – if we have to go I'll leave a note in the summer house. Go!' Jilly said urgently.

Abigail hurried along her secret path through the rhododendrons, taking care that nobody saw her slip through the gate. As she crossed the road by the church, she saw an elderly gentleman coming up Hill Top Road. He was carrying an old fashioned lamp with a glass shade and what looked like a duvet under his arm. He smiled when he passed her and his bright blue eyes twinkled, just like Jilly's.

It's her Grandad, Abigail thought, and she knew she was right.

'Hi everybody!' she called as she went into the vicarage by the back door. 'I feel much better now!'

There was no sign of Matthew and Daniel, even though the table was set for tea. Mr Dutton was sitting at the head of the table, his chin resting on his fingertips, which were pressed together.

Mrs Dutton was leaning on the sink, her face hidden by her dark curly hair and her arms folded. She looked up and her brown eyes were sad.

'Where have you been, Abigail?' she asked, quietly.

Abigail felt her heart fluttering and her stomach turned over.

'I've been to Nicola's,' she lied. There was a long silence and she felt she had to fill it. 'I went for a walk, just on the common, then my headache got better so I went to Nicola's . . . and we played in her garden . . . tennis!'

She could hear her voice shaking but couldn't stop it.

'That's a lie, Abby. Try again,' Mr Dutton said, still looking at his fingertips.

Abigail's heart sank. They knew!

'I've been in Hill House, in the gardens.'

'Oh we know *that*! We've had a visit from your friend Nicola, the one you've been playing tennis with. The question is, why?' Mrs Dutton said.

Abigail tried to keep the tears away but they would keep filling her eyes. Jilly and her Grandparents needed one more night in the shelter of the coach house. What happened then was up to Mr Forbes, the solicitor. She couldn't tell on them, not now!

'Well, Abby, we're waiting?'

She was almost sure her dad would understand. Hadn't he said that people should help those in need? She was tempted to tell him but kept hearing Jilly's voice in her head – 'Please don't tell, oh please don't!'

'I just wanted to look round before it's all gone,' she said. 'I'm sorry, I know I've been trespassing.'

'You shouldn't have gone in there, Abby, you know that. It was wrong, as well as being dangerous, but it's not that I'm disappointed about. It's the lie! The fact that you felt you had to lie about where you'd been. What was the point of that?' Mrs Dutton said.

Abigail couldn't answer and was sent up to bed with a tray. She could hear the boys talking and laughing at the kitchen table and knew that Dad was telling one of his stories. She couldn't help crying and didn't feel like any of the egg salad and brown bread and butter her mum had put on the tray.

'I wish I'd never met Jilly Potts!' she said, miserably, but she didn't really mean it.

Jilly was nice and her grandad looked nice too. It wasn't right that they should have nowhere to live. She thought of Gramps, warm and comfy in his little flat with the whole family to look after him. Who was looking after the Potts and what would happen to them tomorrow?

Abigail wiped her eyes and closed them.

'I'm sorry I lied,' she said aloud, 'But I promised, and they haven't hurt the house. They've made it clean and shiny again, most of it. Please forgive them for trespassing and help them to sort things out. I'll tell Mum and Dad everything after tomorrow, I promise.'

Chapter Eight

Grandad wrapped the candlesticks and the other treasures in pieces of old shirt before putting them back in their brown paper packaging and re-tying the string. He left the faded labels on, too.

'Mr Forbes will want to see the labels, I expect. Better to leave things as you find them, I always say,' he said.

He put the plate and the goblet in Jilly's small suitcase, the candlesticks in Grandma's shopping bag and the cross and altar cloth in a strong plastic carrier bag.

'If I put 'em all in one suitcase I'll never carry it!' he grunted, testing the weight of the bags.

'I'll carry one, Grandad!' Jilly said, lifting her suitcase with two hands. 'Ooh it *is* heavy.'

'Better not, Jilly. I've got these two nicely balanced. It's easier to carry two, when they're balanced, and Grandma can manage the carrier. She's a strong lass!'

'Lass? It's been a long time since I was a lass!' Grandma laughed. 'But I suppose I've still got a bit of strength left in these arms!'

'I'll carry the book. That isn't heavy at all,' Jilly said. 'It'll go in my school bag.'

Jilly emptied the grey and yellow canvas bag that held her pencil case, a rough notebook and last year's timetable. It made her sad, looking at the special things she kept in her school bag.

There was a fluffy imp with wobbly eyes that fitted on the end of a pencil, her collection of rainbow rubbers and a bright purple key ring with a picture of Joseph in his technicolor dreamcoat, in a clear plastic disc. They had all been presents from Cathy, when they were still friends.

Jilly swallowed hard a few times. She didn't want to cry but it looked as if things were going wrong again! Now that they'd found the treasure they'd have to leave Hill House and that meant leaving another friend, just when they were getting to know each other.

Grandad put on his best suit. It had been hanging on the back of the bathroom door since they arrived at the coach house and there weren't *too* many creases in it.

'I look a right mess!' Grandma grumbled as she tried to hide her hair under a silk scarf. 'I haven't had my hair done for weeks!'

'You look fine!' Grandad said. 'You don't look any different now than you did on our wedding day!'

'A likely tale!' Grandma laughed, punching him playfully on the shoulder. 'You'll be telling me I don't look a day over twenty-one next!'

'You don't, to me!' Grandad said, grabbing her and rubbing his bristly chin on her cheek.

'Stop that you silly old thing. I've just put my face on!'

Jilly grinned and all her misery disappeared. Grandad was teasing Grandma and she was enjoying it, even though she was telling him to stop. It was nice being with them because they were happy, in spite of everything, and Jilly felt ashamed of her moans.

Grandma insisted that they tidied the coach house before they left.

'He's not going to turn us out straight away, is he?' Jilly cried. 'Where will we go? What will happen to our things?'

She looked round the room they had made home and at the few things she had saved when they left their own house – a rabbit in a hammock that used to hang in the back of the car, her music box and Mum and Dad's wedding picture in a pink frame.

'We'll cross that bridge when we get to it, Jilly. Mr Forbes is a gentleman, always was, and he'll do his best for us, I'm sure,' Grandad said.

Jilly couldn't help worrying though, especially as they crossed Hill Top Road at the bottom, by the school. There were boys and girls on the playing field and the teacher looked right at her, or seemed to.

'What will Mr Forbes say about me not going to school?' she worried.

'Mr Forbes isn't a school bobby, he's a solicitor! He won't be bothered whether you go to school or not!' Grandad said.

'Where are you living!' Grandma cried. 'They're not called school bobbies these days. They're Education Welfare Officers!'

'I know, I know, and dustbin men are Sanitary Operatives, what's in a name?'

Grandma told him to 'shush' as they joined the bus queue outside the supermarket.

Although it was only a short ride into town, Jilly was tingling with excitement. She hadn't been further than the local shops for ages. It was busy, for a Monday morning, and there were quite a few children about so she didn't feel too out of place on a school day.

The offices of Forbes, Forbes, Miller and Day were in the old part of town, in a row of impressive buildings called 'The Crescent'. Mr Forbes office was on the second floor and there wasn't a lift.

'Phew! I'm not getting any younger in spite of what your grandad thinks, Jilly,' Grandma gasped as they reached the landing. 'I'm glad he isn't on the third floor!'

The lady at reception said that Mr Forbes was with a client at that moment, but made an appointment for them to see him at half past ten.

'Can we leave these?' Grandma asked. 'If I've to climb those stairs again I don't want any bags to carry!'

The lady put the bags between her desk and the filing cabinet.

'What if somebody steals them?' Jilly whispered to Grandma, once they were outside on the landing again.

'Who would want our shopping? Besides, I can't imagine things going missing in a lawyer's office, can you, Grandad?'

Jilly had forgotten that no-one else, except Abigail Dutton, knew what was in the parcels.

It was still only half past nine so they had a good look around the market and a cup of tea at a little snack bar, where Jilly had two slices of toast, dripping with butter.

'I've been dreaming about toast!' she mumbled with her mouth full.

'So that's what all the funny noises were, you grinding your teeth and dreaming about toast?' Grandad cried.

'You make noises too, Grandad. You snore a lot!'

'Snore? Me! Never! I don't snore!'

Grandma spluttered into her tea cup and had to have her back slapped to stop her choking 'Not much you don't!' she gasped, and winked at Jilly.

At half past ten they were ushered into Mr Forbes' office.

'Mr and Mrs Potts, how nice to see you again!' he said, leaning over his desk to shake their hands. 'And can this be your grand-daughter? You were just a baby last time we met, Miss Potts!'

Jilly grinned at being called Miss Potts. She liked Mr Forbes right away.

'Do sit down,' he said, pointing to an extra chair for Jilly. 'Do you know. I've missed your gran's cherry cake. There was always a piece put out for me when I visited Mr Lyle. Now, what can I do for you?'

Jilly watched Mr Forbes' face as Grandad told their story. She saw his concern about the loss of Dad's business and his anger when he heard about the bed and breakfast place. He looked shocked when Grandad told him they'd been living in the coach house.

'But the power's disconnected, no heat and light!' he said.

'We've managed,' Grandad insisted. 'And we've cleaned the place up a bit too – couldn't bear to see it so neglected. I know we're squatting, but we just couldn't stand the place we were living in, the indignity of it all – and Hill House was our home, for most of our lives.'

'I don't know what to say, Mr Potts. No-one knew you were there so why have you come to me now? You know I'll have to act on the matter, now I'm in the picture!' Mr Forbes said, shaking his head.

'Because of these!' Grandad said, opening the bags and putting the parcels on the green leather top of the desk.

'Whatever? . . . MY WORD!' Mr Forbes gasped, when he saw what was in the packages. 'Where did you find these?'

'They were in the drawing room windowseat, not

that it was really a seat, just a deep sill really. It was all nailed up and painted over and hadn't been opened for nigh on a hundred years, I'd say. Sarah and Jilly were doing a bit of cleaning and came across the parcels.'

'It was because of the mice!' Jilly explained, and Mr Forbes looked so puzzled that Grandad started again, from the beginning.

When Mr Forbes saw the ledger and the inventory he was really excited.

'There's a whole list of things here and only a few ticked off!' he cried. 'This changes things quite a bit!'

Jilly gulped. Mr Forbes had been very nice and understanding – so far! Was he going to be angry now that he'd seen the treasure?

'Mr Yates, the Hill Top builder, has made an offer for the property,' he went on, 'but we are no further ahead than we were six years ago! I have recently contacted, by letter, a Mr Lyle-Travers of Toronto, Canada, who is, I believe, the great-nephew we've been looking for. I've already informed Mr Yates of this new development, and the possibility that an heir could make a difference to the fate of Hill House. Until I hear from Canada I think we'd better leave things as they are!'

'You mean we can go on living in the coach house?' Grandad asked.

'I don't see why not! As executor of the Lyle estate I have the authority to sanction that.'

'That's mega!' Jilly cried.

'Mega? Is that a modern way of saying "super-duper," young lady?' Mr Forbes said, smiling.

'It was "spiffing" and "wizard" in my day!' Grandad said.

'We really are grateful, Mr Forbes. It's like being back

home again – almost!' Grandma said, her face beaming with delight.

'I think I can make it even more like home! Give me a few moments!' Mr Forbes said, leaving them while he went to talk to his secretary.

'I knew it would be all right,' Grandad sighed. 'He always was a gentleman.'

'And we can live in the coach house, properly?' Jilly asked.

'We can – at least, until this nephew turns up and decides what to do with the place. I don't remember him at all!' Grandad said, shaking his head as he tried to think back.

'I can't wait to tell Abigail!' Jilly cried.

'Who?'

Grandma and Grandad said 'who' together and Jilly's heart missed a beat. Now she'd done it!

Just then Mr Forbes came hurrying in and, for the moment, Jilly didn't have to answer the question 'who'!

'Now! The electricity board will be with you at two-thirty this afternoon, that will give you light, heat and hot water, and I've authorised the removal of anything you need from the repository. Some of the antiques have gone and the rest are stored privately, but most of the ordinary household goods are stored there. Here is a letter of authorisation and the address – take what you need to make yourselves comfortable, and if you have any problems – I'll be here all day.'

'I don't know what to say!' Grandad began, but Mr Forbes held up his hand.

'Don't say anything Mr Potts. There are those who would have kept the treasures to themselves, and then they would have been lost to the estate. Besides, there is a chance there's more hidden about the place. I'd like somebody on the premises!'

At twelve o'clock Jilly was in a phone box in the market square and her mum and dad heard all about Hill House, the treasure, and Mr Forbes.

'That's wonderful news, Jilly!' Dad said. 'And our news is good too! Mum and I have a nice room and we're both working hard. It won't be long before we're on our feet again, and all together.'

It made Jilly cry a bit, talking to her mum and dad who were so far away, but there was so much to do that she had to stop thinking about them and help Grandma and Grandad to get organised.

The repository was huge and there was furniture everywhere, piled high in numbered bays.

'This is the Lyle bay,' a man in a boiler suit said, showing them to the back of a large warehouse. 'Point out the stuff you want to 'Arry 'ere and we'll 'ave it with you by tea-time!'

Harry was a tall young man with a ponytail who winked at Jilly and gave her a tiny pink pottery pig.

'Take him home with you, kid. I can't stand his grunts!'

Jilly grinned her thanks and put the pig in her bag. Everyone was being so nice.

'What do you want then?' Harry went on, waving his arm towards the pile behind him.

'A sofa, that green one over there, a chair to match if there is one and a couple of beds, a double and a single. Is there any bedding?' Grandad asked.

'We've even got the coat hangers and dusters in 'ere mister. When we do a house clearance we bring the lot! There'll be curtains and blankets sealed in polythene somewhere round here. Anything else?'

'A carpet for the living room, and a couple of chests

of drawers would be useful,' Grandma said.

'And that standard lamp!'

'And that bedside table.'

'Is that a fridge?'

'Well I never, that's my old cooker!'

'Can I have a little lamp for my room, and a rug?' Jilly asked.

It was very exciting and Harry wrote everything down on a clipboard and put a red label on things that were 'to go'.

'Can we get the lorry up the drive?' he asked.

'I should think there'll be a key on this bunch,' Grandad said, shaking the keys that Mr Forbes had given him. 'And there's tarmac all the way up the drive, it's only weed that's covering it.'

Grandad promised to open the main gates as they left and it wasn't until they were on the bus back to Hill Top that Grandma remembered Abigail.

'Who's this girl you mentioned, Jilly?' she asked.

She was sitting beside Jilly and Grandad was on the seat in front. He turned round to hear what was going on.

'She's the girl I told you about, the one I met in the lane.'

'You didn't tell us you'd been talking to her, Jilly! How much does she know?'

Jilly hung her head and tried to stop her mouth turning down at the corners.

'Everything,' she said softly.

'I don't believe it Jilly! It doesn't matter now, as it happens, but you didn't know all this was going to happen. It could have been serious if she'd told anyone!'

'She didn't! She wouldn't, she promised.'

'You shouldn't ask people to make promises like that, Jilly. It means that she was doing wrong too. It's called aiding and abetting and is just as serious! Who is this young lady? We'd better put her straight before she lands herself in trouble!' Grandad said.

He was cross, and Jilly knew that it was her he was angry with, for involving somebody else.

'Abigail Dutton,' she said. 'She lives at the vicarage.'

'That's the vicar's little girl, I remember her!' Grandma said. 'A serious little thing she was, with big brown eyes. Oh Jilly – you've not had the vicar's daughter keeping secrets?'

Jilly had begun to cry.

'I'm sorry,' she sobbed, trying to explain. 'She followed me and I had to tell her. She did promise not to tell. I'm meeting her in the summer house after she comes home from school, so I'll tell her it's not a secret any more.'

'That's not the point, love, is it? How is she going to admit that she knew all along? You've put her in an awful position!' Grandad sighed.

Nothing more was said as the bus chugged to Hill Top and they walked up Hill Top Road in silence. Grandad unlocked the double gates to the drive and opened them wide. It didn't matter whether they were seen or not now.

It began to rain as they reached the coach house and the sky was very dark and menacing. The trees were rustling and swaying and it looked as if a thunder storm wasn't far away.

'I thought this good weather was too good to be true!' Grandad muttered.

The man from the electricity board turned the power

on and promised to send somebody to fit the cooker at tea-time.

'You'd better go and put a note in the summer house,' Grandma said. 'It's not raining much at the moment but it's too nasty to wait for your friend at the gate. Leave a note telling her to come here, for tea. I expect she has a secret path to the summer house?'

Jilly nodded. 'There's a secret path!'

'Well it's time all secrets were out in the open!' Grandma said.

It was raining quite heavily as Jilly hurried to the summer house and there was a flash of lightning as she put her note on the orange box and kept it in place with an old plant pot. Perhaps Abigail wouldn't come, in the rain, but if she did she'd find the note and come to the coach house.

'If she doesn't come today, I'll wait outside school tomorrow. Won't she be surprised?' Jilly said to no-one in particular as she hurried back indoors.

The lights were on, because of the storm, and it really did look like home, all lit up to welcome her.

Chapter Nine

Abigail was late. She hadn't slept very well and felt quite ill when she sat down to breakfast.

'Can I just have some toast, please?' she said, gulping at the thought of a runny egg.

'You need a good breakfast inside you when you're at school!' Mrs Dutton said. 'You need food for energy!'

'I eat lots of breakfast so I've got plenty of energy!' Daniel announced, dipping his 'soldier' in his egg with such force that the yellow yolk sploshed over and ran down the shell onto his plate.

'Do be careful, Daniel!' Mrs Dutton scolded, as he wiped his plate with another strip of toast. 'And keep your tie out of the way!'

Abigail sliced the top off her egg and spooned a mouthful out of the shell.

'I really can't eat it, Mum,' she said softly.

'Well leave it then! I don't know what's the matter with you lately, Abigail. You're not yourself, that's for sure. Is there something bothering you?' Mrs Dutton said, removing the egg and giving it to Daniel who had his hand up, asking for it.

'It's just that – there's something – I haven't . . .' Abigail stammered.

'Spit it out Abby, it might be a gold watch!' Mr

Dutton cried, standing up and trying to peer down Abigail's throat.

'Why would it be a gold watch?' Matthew asked, his nose wrinkled in disbelief.

'Why not? There's obviously something very important in there if it takes so much getting out, and a gold watch is a very important thing to have! Shall I dig around in there, Abby?' Mr Dutton teased, pulling Abigail's chin down to open her mouth and brandishing his butter knife.

'It's not that important,' Abigail sighed when her dad had let go of her chin. It was so hard to tell what she was worried about. She could hear Jilly's voice inside her head – 'Please don't tell, oh please don't tell!' – and she couldn't let her down.

'I'm just sorry I lied to you, about where I'd been. I'm very, very sorry,' she said.

'Now Abby-Dabby-Doo, that's over and done with so forget it. This family doesn't keep on and on about things, does it? It's history!' Mr Dutton said.

But it wasn't, Abigail set off for school with it all still on her mind and had to face a flurry of angry ducks who were waiting for breakfast.

'Well I just forgot!' she told them grumpily. 'I can't remember everything!'

She even forgot to wait for Katie-Marie, who had to run hard to catch up with her.

'What's the matter with you this morning? Why didn't you wait?' she asked, angrily.

'I'm sorry, I didn't think,' Abigail said, trying to smile at Katie-Marie, then frowning again as they approached Nicola. 'Thanks a lot, Nicola!' she added as she walked past.

'Well! You told a lie – you said you were going home!'

Nicola snapped.

'Is that why you followed me?' Abigail asked, hurrying down Hill Top Road.

'What's up? What's happened?' Katie-Marie asked, running and skipping to keep up with the pair of them.

'Ask her!' Abigail growled, before darting across the crossing and in through the gates, ignoring Claire who was waiting as usual.

'She went into Hill House . . . After all she said, *"It's trespassing"* that's what she said, but it's all right for HER!' Nicola said spitefully.

'When? When did she go in?' Katie-Marie asked.

'Yesterday afternoon!'

'I called for her to come out with me and my stepdad. She said she wasn't feeling well!' Katie-Marie said indignantly.

'Well she was all right to go trespassing in Hill House!' Nicola said. 'I went and told her dad!'

'You didn't!'

'I did!'

'That was really mean, Niki!' Claire said.

'It's nothing to do with you!' Nicola said, tossing her ponytail and marching into school.

'It serves her right if she got into trouble. She shouldn't tell lies!' Katie-Marie said, following Nicola and tossing *her* head too.

It was not a good start to the day.

Miss Newton was quite concerned because she could see that something was wrong. The class went into the hall for games because it was raining, and when they had to find a partner, Abigail and Nicola went to opposite ends of the room. Katie-Marie went to Nicola and Claire went to Abigail, when it was usually the other way round! Miss Newton could see there had been a quarrel.

The period after PE was always set aside as a quiet time, when Miss Newton read to the class or asked them to read a favourite poem or tell about a hobby or an interest. Today she decided to let the boys and girls do the talking.

'Has anybody anything interesting to tell the class?' she asked.

Several hands shot up and Miss Newton pointed to Jason Bennet who hurried to the front.

'On Saturday I went to a theme park . . .' he began excitedly.

Abigail wasn't listening. She felt too miserable to be bothered with tales of roller coasters and ghost trains. Katie-Marie was still sitting in the desk next to hers but had twisted right round so she was facing Nicola. She wouldn't even look at Abigail!

'Don't mind them!' Claire whispered. 'They're being stupid and mean!'

Abigail shook her head. 'It was my fault, I did lie to Nicola and . . .'

Before she had time to finish, Nicola leaned forward and poked Abigail. 'Don't talk about me behind my back!' she hissed.

'She wasn't!' Claire said loudly. 'She was just – '

'Just one minute, please!' Miss Newton sounded angry and Claire closed her mouth. 'I think there's something going on that needs sorting out! Thank you Jason, that was very interesting. Claire, have you something to tell us?'

There was a long, uncomfortable silence. Claire just sat with a silly grin on her face, Abigail studied an ink stain on her desk lid, Katie-Marie stared out of the window and Nicola stared at Miss Newton.

'Well?' the teacher asked again.

'It's my fault,' Abigail sighed. 'I did something I shouldn't and – '

'And Nicola told on her!' Claire butted in.

'She went into Hill House garden when *she* was the one who said we shouldn't because it's trespassing. And she told a lie!' Nicola protested. 'It's wrong to tell lies, isn't it Miss Newton?'

'It is, in most cases, Nicola. I suppose there are times when telling a lie could be the right thing to do,' Miss Newton said.

Everbody gasped and even Abigail lifted her head to stare at the teacher. When would it be all right to tell a lie?

'Imagine,' Miss Newton went on. 'Imagine you have just arrived home after a busy day at school. You've just put your feet up with a cup of hot chocolate when the doorbell rings. It's old Mrs Brown from next door and she wants you to run down to the shops – if it's no trouble and you're not doing anything important – Abigail, what would you say?'

'I'd say it was no trouble and go on the errand.'

'And would that be the truth?'

'Well, no! I wouldn't want to but . . .'

'So you'd be telling a lie, an untruth?' Miss Newton suggested.

'I suppose so. But that's not the same, is it?'

'Isn't it? Isn't not telling the truth the same as telling a lie?'

'No!' Abigail said. 'If I told Mrs Brown how I really felt, that she was a nuisance and I didn't want to go, she'd be so hurt.'

'Ah! So we can tell untruths to save somebody from

being hurt, can we?' Miss Newton asked the class.

Abigail was very thoughtful and hardly listened to the next bit about telling lies. She had a question to ask and it needed thinking out first.

'Suppose someone told you a secret and it meant telling lies to keep it?' she asked. 'What if you promised your friend something, something important. Isn't it right to keep your promise, even if it means telling lies?'

'You never promised me anything!' Nicola said.

'Not you. Somebody I just met!'

Abigail began to feel very hot and uncomfortable. Everyone was looking at her and wondering what she meant.

Miss Newton always seemed to answer a question with another question. 'Suppose you had a friend, a best friend, who was doing something really silly and dangerous – like sniffing glue?'

'Yuk!' Martin grunted. 'We had a film about that. It's stupid!'

'It is Martin, but some boys and girls do it. Well Abigail, suppose your best friend told you she was sniffing glue, and made you promise not to tell, would you be a good friend if you kept the secret?'

'No,' Abigail said. 'A true friend would tell and get help, before something awful happened.'

'That's right, Abigail. Sometimes we have to hurt our friends to help them.'

'But what if – what if nobody would be hurt? What if the promise is just for a little while until something is sorted out and it would really, really help somebody?' Abigail said.

Miss Newton shook her head. 'Without knowing the details it's hard to say, Abigail, but in that case I would say it's a matter for the friend to use her own judgement.

The trouble is, helping one friend can mean deceiving another!'

There was another upset, at break, when Abigail refused to say what she had been talking about.

'It's about that girl you said you saw, isn't it?' Nicola demanded.

'No it isn't!' Abigail cried. 'Leave me alone!'

'We will!' Katie-Marie said, grabbing Nicola's arm and dragging her away.

'Do you want me to go away, too?' Claire asked.

'Do what you want!'

Claire shrugged her shoulders and followed the others, leaving Abigail by the cloakroom door, alone and miserable.

By lunchtime, the wind was really strong and although the rain had stopped for a while, there were dark clouds gathering overhead and by hometime the whole sky was dark and threatening.

Mrs Dutton was at the school gates waiting with Matthew and Daniel. 'Hurry up, Abigail,' she said. 'This storm's going to break any minute!' and as she said it there was a flash of lightning and a loud thunderclap.

'Four seconds! It's only four miles away!' Matthew cried gleefully. He liked a good storm.

'If we hurry we'll get home before it pours. It's going to be a big storm!' Mrs Dutton said.

'You go on!' Abigail suggested, anxious about her meeting with Jilly. 'I'll wait for Katie-Marie.'

'No you won't! Katie-Marie's already gone in Nicola's car. Hurry!'

There was no point in arguing. Abigail held David's other hand and the four almost ran up Hill Top Road, past the pond and through the church yard. The lightning was flashing and the thunder was crashing and big heavy drops started to fall just as they reached the kitchen door.

Abigail ran straight upstairs and hurried to her bedroom window. The big trees behind the high red-brick wall were swaying from side to side as the strong wind caught their branches and the flashes of lightning, almost continuous now, lit up the wet, grey roof of Hill House itself.

For a fleeting moment Abigail thought she saw Jilly's blonde head bobbing in the bushes round the summer house, then the clouds burst and amidst the roar of thunder the rain lashed the windowpanes and obscured her view.

Abigail gulped. At least Jilly would have some shelter in the summer house, if the roof didn't leak!

The vicarage kitchen was warm and cosy even though the noise of the storm kept making everybody jump. Mrs Dutton filled the children's plates with hot spaghetti on toast and opened the stove doors to warm the room. Mr Dutton came in from his study when they were halfway through tea and joined them for his share.

'You're quiet!' he said. 'I suppose the thunder is talking enough for everybody!'

'It's really close!' Matthew said. 'I'd like to go out and watch it, I like lightning!'

Daniel didn't say anything. He was trying to suck up a long string of spaghetti.

'Don't do that, Daniel!' Mrs Dutton said and just as she spoke there was another terrific crash and Daniel's spaghetti shot into his mouth and nearly choked him!

'That was *really* close!' Matthew said, a little more quietly.

Abigail felt as if she was seeing things in slow motion, like in a dream. Mrs Dutton was slapping Daniel's back to remove the spaghetti, Mr Dutton was buttering his extra toast and Matthew was waving his fork at the window where the rain lashed down. She wanted to scream that Jilly was out in the storm but the words wouldn't come.

There was a flash, brighter than all the others, and at the same time a tremendous clap of thunder that seemed to shake the house and everybody in it.

Abigail jumped to her feet and made for the door, Matthew dropped his fork and Daniel's spaghetti shot out of his throat and splattered the milk jug.

'That hit something . . . close!' Mr Dutton cried, hurrying to the kitchen door to see if his church still had a spire!

Abigail took the stairs two at a time, her heart thumping in her chest. Across Hill Rise the trees had stopped swaying, the rain had lessened a little and . . .

Something was wrong, different, and with a cry that carried all the way down to the kitchen, Abigail realised that the big horsechestnut – the candle tree – was down, snapped like a twig just above the height of the wall. She could see a lot more of Hill House now and something else – where was the rusty cockerel that sat on top of the summer house? Where was the summer house? All she could see was the broken tree where the summer house had stood.

'Jilly!'

She screamed Jilly's name just as Mr and Mrs Dutton hurried into her bedroom.

'Abigail what is it? What's wrong?'

'Jilly! – It's Jilly – Jilly's in the summer house!'

Chapter Ten

The rain had stopped, although the thunder was still rumbling in the distance. Abigail followed Mr Dutton across Hill Rise and up the long drive to Hill House. It wasn't until they were through the main gates that she realised they were open. There were tyre tracks too, big ones that had crushed the carpet of moss and trailing weeds that covered the tarmac.

Somebody was already in there! Was it the police? Abigail's heart was pounding as they neared the house and almost stopped when she saw the lights in the coach house. The rooms over the row of garages were ablaze with light, electric light, and the curtains weren't even drawn to hide them! Something terrible had happened, she was sure it had.

'Well? Where's this summer house?' Mr Dutton said sternly.

At first, when Abigail had screamed Jilly's name, he had been concerned and as worried for her safety as Abigail was. Then, as she sobbed out the whole story, including the fact that she had arranged to meet Jilly in the summer house, he had become angry.

'How many times have you been warned about wandering off into lonely places? What have we taught you about honesty and truthfulness? What were you thinking about, concealing a crime? Trespassing *is* a crime, Abigail, and here you are aiding and abetting criminals! We'd better call the police!'

He just wouldn't let Abigail speak, he was so angry. Matthew and Daniel had disappeared to their rooms, in case they'd done something wrong. Mr Dutton didn't lose his temper very often but when he did, it was time to have something very important to do, somewhere else!

Abigail tried to tell him that Jilly and her grandparents weren't criminals and that Jilly was her friend and a very nice person, but he kept on and on about strangers and derelict houses until she had stamped on the floor and screamed . . .

'NO! LISTEN!'

Mr Dutton was so surprised at the outburst from quiet, thoughtful Abigail that he did listen and when he realised that the trespassers were his old friends Mr and Mrs Potts and not a band of cut-throat villains he stopped shouting.

'Right,' he'd said. 'We'll have the whole story, but firstly, we'd better see if your friend is safe. But if she has any sense at all she'll have been indoors all afternoon, and nowhere near the summer house!'

Abigail had gone with him, to show him how to get in the back gate, but they'd both walked up the drive without thinking because the front gates were wide open.

Now, with her dad asking to go to the summer house, Abigail didn't know what to do for the best.

'Should we go to their house first,' she said, looking at the garages and the light above them, 'in case she's there?'

Mr Dutton nodded and they hurried across the overgrown lawns and up the outside staircase. The door was wide open and there was a TV at the side of the fireplace. It was showing cartoons and Daffy Duck was making a lot of noise as he was being chased by a hunter. There were chairs and a settee, a lovely log fire was burning in the grate and the table was laid for tea.

Abigail didn't know what to think. It wasn't a bit like Jilly had described. Where was the old sun lounger and the little camping stove? Where were the faded deck chairs that Grandma and Grandad slept in?

'This doesn't look like somebody camping in secret, Abby, does it?' Mr Dutton said.

Abigail tried not to cry, though she felt like it. Had it all been lies, all of it?

'Something must have happened,' she said. 'Jilly wouldn't lie to me.'

'You lied to me and Mum, Abby. Didn't you?'

Abigail nodded. She had lied to protect Jilly, to help her family who were in trouble. She thought of the Sunday service and her dad asking them to think of the less fortunate. *"I tell you indeed, whenever you did this for one of the least important of these brothers of mine, you did it for me."* She could still hear her father saying that.

'I only wanted to help, to be the sort of Christian Jesus wants me to be, like you said. I wouldn't have had to lie if Nicola hadn't told on me,' she said softly.

'We'll have to have a long talk, you and I Abby-Dabby!' Mr Dutton said, putting his arm round her shoulders. 'Think about it – is not telling the truth different from telling a lie?'

'Yes . . . no . . . yes . . . I don't know!'

'We'll talk about it later. Let's go and find this friend of yours,' Mr Dutton said.

'Something's happened and I'm sure Jilly will explain, when we find her,' Abigail said as they set off.

The secret path through the rhododendrons was muddy after the heavy rain and every leaf seemed to be holding a little pool of water that showered droplets on them as they squelched through the undergrowth.

'It's lovely when it's sunny,' Abigail said, almost to herself.

'Humph!' Mr Dutton answered as another deluge landed on his head.

As they neared the summer house Abigail's heart started thumping again. What if Jilly was inside when the tree fell? What if she was trapped and Grandad was trying to get her out? What if she was hurt and they'd all rushed off to hospital in an ambulance? What if . . .?

Mr and Mrs Potts were standing by the broken tree and Jilly was with them!

'Jilly!' Abigail cried, running across the clearing to hug her friend. 'I saw you near the summer house then the tree fell. I thought you were under it!'

Jilly was hugging Abigail and beaming all over her face.

'I left you a note and we were just going to have tea when we heard it. I thought *you* were in there!'

'And that's where both of you might have been, if we hadn't got things sorted out!' Mr Potts said, nodding towards the wreckage. 'Just look at that!'

The summer house was gone! The top half of the huge horse-chestnut had crashed right down on it. The branches were entangled with the wrought iron frame and another tree, a sycamore. It had been brought down by the weight of the candle tree and its roots had lifted right out of the ground. Between them were broken pieces of black and white marble, the broken tiles of the summer house floor.

'The floor's gone!' Abigail gasped. 'The tree's lifted the floor up!'

It was true and Mr Dutton went forward with Mr Potts to investigate. The girls started after them but Mr Dutton was firm.

'You two stay right there for the moment!'

Abigail and Jilly watched as Mr Dutton picked his way between the tree roots and broken flags.

'Well I never!' Mr Potts said slowly, letting his breath out as he spoke.

Abigail, hopping from one foot to the other, couldn't contain herself any longer and hurried to join her dad.

'What is it, Daddy?' she asked, leaning over to peer into the dark hole that had appeared.

'We're not sure Abby-Dabby. It looks as if there's something underneath,' he said.

Abigail grinned at Jilly and beckoned her to come forward. Being called her pet name, twice, meant that her dad had started to forgive her and he wasn't *quite* so angry any more.

Between the roots of the old sycamore was a hollow, like a cellar, or a well. Abigail could see that the walls were made of stone and not just earth. Beneath the black and white tiles were pieces of much older stone, great slabs of it as big as table tops. One of them had cracked and fallen into the darkness below. Even as they peered down into the gloom, the tree shifted a little and another piece fell into the depths.

'Is it a well?' Abigail whispered.

'Can't tell, lovey,' Mr Potts said, stroking his chin. 'And now's not the time to find out!' He looked up at the sky as he spoke. The dark clouds were gathering again and distant rumbles threatened more rain that night. 'Come on, let's all have a cup of tea and think about all this!'

'What's happened?' Abigail whispered as the girls followed the grown-ups back to the coach house.

'Everything, it's wonderful!' Jilly grinned, linking arms with Abigail as good friends should.

It wasn't very far but Abigail had most of the story by the time they reached the stairs.

'So you can stay here?' she cried excitedly.

'Yes, isn't it MEGA! And Grandad's going to see about school tomorrow!'

'My school? You're coming to *my* school?'

'If I can! Isn't it great? And Mum and Dad are getting on fine as well, everything's great!'

Jilly stopped when she heard Abigail sigh.

'Are you in a lot of trouble?' she asked.

'A bit,' Abigail nodded. 'I shouldn't have lied.'

'It's my fault, I'm sorry,' Jilly said.

'It's my own fault!' Abigail insisted. 'It's not about keeping secrets, not really. It's about not trusting Mummy and Daddy with the truth. They would have helped, I know they would. Daddy's cross because I lied to him – didn't trust him.'

'You wouldn't have had to lie at all if it wasn't for me,' Jilly sighed.

'Well I did, and it's done now. I suppose I'll be punished but I deserve it so I won't mind, honestly. Besides, everything's come right for you so let's forget about it, for now,' Abigail said, smiling as she took Jilly's hand to run up the steps.

It was cosy, having hot drinks in the comfy coach house. The furniture, the log fire and a nice carpet had made a lot of difference and two pretty lamps cast a warm glow on the assembled company. Mr Dutton chatted to Mr and Mrs Potts about the old days, when the estate was well kept and lived in, and heard about the problems his old friends had been having. He heard about the treasure that had come to light too.

'And now there's that big hole!' Mr Potts said. 'I wonder what we'll find down there.'

'I bet there's more treasure!' Abigail cried. 'I can't wait to look!'

'You'll wait a long time, young lady, at least a week! You're grounded!' Mr Dutton said sternly.

'But – ' Abigail began.

'But nothing! You know the rules, Abby. You didn't expect everything to be forgotten, just like that!'

'I'll keep away too,' Jilly said. 'It wouldn't be fair.'

'I know you will, Jilly Potts! You did your share of fibbing too! It's school, then straight home for a week, at least!' Grandad said, shaking his finger at Jilly.

Abigail and Jilly looked at each other and sighed.

'At least we'll be together at school!' Abigail said.

But they weren't. Jilly had to go into Mr Latchem's class because Miss Newton had thirty-two children already.

They did manage to meet up at break and at lunchtime and Claire and Katie-Marie liked Jilly straight away. Katie-Marie forgot all about her quarrel with Abigail as they listened to the exciting news about Hill House and its treasure. Nicola was not so ready to forgive and forget.

'You've stopped my father from buying that land!' she accused Jilly.

'I didn't do anything of the sort,' Jilly said. 'It was Hill House itself that did it, by showing us its treasure.'

'Rubbish!' Nicola sneered, but she gathered round to hear the story, just like the others.

By the end of the punishment week Abigail was bursting to know what was going on. Jilly could tell her a bit but it *was* only a bit because she wasn't allowed near the summer house either.

Straight after tea and for as long as it was light enough to see, Abigail had been glued to her bedroom window. There was lots of movement. Great machines lifted the broken trees and buzzing saws cut the branches into pieces before they were loaded onto lorries and carted away. Then a large caravan appeared. She could just see its roof and funnel-chimney peeping above the rhododendrons. Mr Dutton said that an archaeological team had arrived to investigate.

'It's just a hole. Why would they be interested in a hole?' Matthew asked.

'It isn't just a hole, Matthew,' Mr Dutton explained. 'It's an underground room. We could see a bit of the ribbed vaulting through the first opening and in the light of what's already been found, I'd think it's very interesting!'

At last it was Saturday and the ban was lifted. Abigail ran up the drive ahead of Mr Dutton, who was as keen as she was to see what was happening.

Jilly was sitting on the coach house stairs.

'I waited for you,' she said, jumping to her feet as soon as she saw Abigail running towards her. 'It wouldn't be fair to see it before you do.'

The site was a bit of a mess and part of Abigail was sad that the lovely trees, the old summer house and the flagged space in front of it was gone, but most of her was very excited.

The team of investigators had removed all of the broken summer house, except the rusty cockerel which sat on top of their caravan now. The stone flags were gone as well as a huge pile of earth that had fallen from the tree roots. The hole was now the entrance to a hidden room and there were worn stone steps leading down into it.

Mr Forbes was at the site and Jilly smiled when he waved at her.

'That's Mr Forbes,' she told Abigail. 'He's really nice.'

'I wonder if he'll let us go down and look?' Abigail said.

'I'll ask him!' Jilly cried and in two minutes she was calling Abigail to the top of the steps.

It was very dark, down under the earth. Mr Gilbey, the leader of the excavation team, helped the girls down the worn stone steps until they were standing on a stone-flagged floor.

'It's like a cellar!' Jilly cried. 'We had one at our old house.'

'But look at the roof!' Abigail said softly.

'Why are you whispering?' Jilly asked.

'Because – I don't know, it seems right somehow.'

'That's because it's a special place, Abby, a very special place.'

Mr Dutton was touching the stone-clad walls as he spoke and he was smiling.

'It makes me feel peaceful. It's not at all scary, is it?' Jilly said.

'It's a little church, isn't it?' Abigail whispered. 'That's why it feels so special, it's a place of worship!'

Mr Dutton put his hand on Abigail's shoulder and

squeezed it gently, as if to say, 'You're right, Abby.'

'But why is it hidden under the ground?' Jilly said, following the light of Mr Gilbey's torch as it beamed across the vaulted ceiling and down the back wall.

'It *is* a church, isn't it?' Abigail said.

'That's right,' Mr Dutton nodded. 'It's a place of worship. Look at that little niche over there. That's where the altar plate and cup would have been.'

'Not would have been – Were!' Mr Gilbey said. 'They're in the caravan with some other finds. I'll show you if you like.'

'What's that?' Jilly said, pointing to a dark patch right in the corner of the back wall.

Mr Gilbey shone his torch and led them across the floor. 'It's a tunnel. We haven't cleared it yet but I suspect it leads into the woods, or what would have been woods centuries ago,' he said. 'Come on, I'll show you what we've found.'

Mr Forbes was looking at the things when the little group entered the caravan. There were two more candlesticks, a large cross, a cup on a long stem with red stones in a band round the rim, a strange bowl with chains, and an oblong piece of wood that looked very old and crumbly.

'A censer,' Mr Dutton said, picking up the bowl with the chains. 'Or a "thurible" if you prefer to call it that.'

'What's it for?' Jilly asked.

'For burning sweet-smelling incense during worship.'

'And what's that?' Abigail asked, pointing to the old piece of wood.

Mr Forbes handled it very carefully, opening it out so she could see that it was really three pieces of wood, hinged so it could be folded. It was like a little screen that could stand on its own when it was opened out.

On it were three paintings, rather faded and grimy, but still very beautiful. The one on the left showed Mary holding the holy baby. The right one showed Jesus, crucified on Calvary, and in the middle, most beautiful of all, was Jesus, ascending to his father in heaven and surrounded by angels.

'It's very old,' Mr Forbes said. 'It must have been hidden here more than four hundred years ago, but it's much older than that.'

'But why?' Jilly persisted. 'Why did they have to be hidden away under the ground?'

'It's a long story,' Mr Dutton said. 'What do you know about Henry the Eighth?'

'He had six wives, but not all at once,' Jilly grinned.

'He was married to Catherine of Aragon but he wanted a divorce to marry Anne Boleyn,' Abigail added. 'I saw it on TV.'

'Catherine gave him a daughter, Mary, but he wanted a son to be king after him.' Mr Dutton explained. 'The church was ruled by Rome at the time and divorce was forbidden, so Henry broke away from Rome and formed the Church of England, with himself as its head, then he could make his own rules. He divorced Catherine and married Anne Boleyn, who also had a daughter, Elizabeth.'

'Elizabeth the First!' Abigail cried.

'But why did they have to hide the little church?' Jilly said. 'I still don't understand!'

Mr Forbes took up the story then.

'Henry had two daughters. He did have a son, later, but he didn't live very long and Elizabeth became queen.'

'Why didn't Mary become queen, she was the oldest?' Abigail said. 'It doesn't seem very fair!'

'Mary was out of favour. She was a Catholic, a follower of the Church of Rome, while Elizabeth was a Protestant, a follower of the Church of England.'

'What does "Catholic" mean?' Jilly asked.

'It means "Universal", for all people. The trouble was that all the services were in Latin, the language of Rome, and most of the people didn't know what was going on. Worship was a great mystery to all but the priests. That's when the protestors or Protestants, like Martin Luther and Wyclif, translated everything into English, so that everyone could understand Jesus' message to all people.'

'But why did they have to hide?' Jilly persisted.

'Look at this,' Mr Gilbey said. 'It's from Sir John Haywards Annals of the first four years of Queen Elizabeth . . . 1559.'

Jilly and Abigail leant forward to look at the book Mr Gilbey was holding.

"Not only images, but roode-lofts, relickes, sepulchres, bookes, banneres, coopes, vestements, altar cloathes wer in diverse places committed to the fire, and that with shouting and applause," they read.

'What funny spelling!' Jilly said.

'Isn't it,' Abigail agreed. 'I can understand what a relic is, and a banner . . . but what's a rood loft?'

'And a coope?' Jilly added.

'Rood is the old English word for cross, and one would be high up on top of the screen that divided the chancel from the nave in a medieval church. The cross would be in the loft, so to speak!' Mr Gilbey explained.

'And a coope, or cope, in present day language, is a large cloak worn by clergy on ceremonial occasions,' Mr Dutton said.

'So Elizabeth stopped the Catholics from worshipping the way they wanted to,' Abigail said thoughtfully. 'But they still did, in secret!'

'Truly! They celebrated Mass in Latin, in hidden rooms and underground tunnels. It was punishable by death if they were caught, or even if they were caught hiding priests!'

'I've heard of priest's holes,' Jilly cried. 'I went to a big old house once, with school, and there was a hidey-hole under the stairs. Just big enough for a man to squeeze into. Michael Barret got in to try it and he said it was really scary! Mrs Drury said it was a priest hole but I was right at the back and didn't hear the rest of it.'

'Didn't you ask?' Abigail said, amazed. 'I would have!'

'I wasn't interested in old houses then. I am now though,' Jilly grinned.

'Here's another bit you might find interesting,' Mr Gilbey said. 'It's from the biography of one John Gerrard, a priest. . . .

" *Braddocks 1594.*

On Easter Monday, as we were preparing everything for Mass before daybreak we heard, suddenly, a great noise of galloping hooves. The next moment . . . the house was surrounded by a whole troop of men.

We barred the doors, the altar was stripped, the hiding places opened and all my books and papers thrown in. It was most important to pack me away first, with all my belongings. I was for using the hiding place near the dining room; it was further away from the chapel, the most suspected room in the house, and it had a supply of provisions . . . However, the Mistress of the house was opposed to it. She wanted me to use the place near the chapel, I could get into it more easily and hide all the altar things with me. As she was very insistent I agreed, although I knew I would have nothing to eat if the search was a long one. We hid away everything that needed hiding."

'It goes on to describe the search, how all the walls were tapped to see if they were hollow and how they knocked down any that were suspicious.'

'It must have been awful for the priests, shut up in the dark like that and hearing the soldiers banging on the walls!' Abigail said.

Mr Forbes started to unroll some large sheets of paper, choosing one covered in drawings.

'These are the plans of the present house,' he explained, smoothing out the sheet on top of Mr Gilbey's table. 'As you can see, the dotted outline, over here to the west, is the site of the original Elizabethan house! It must have stood right over the summer house site, putting the underground church about here, under the kitchens!'

'I read about that!' Abigail interrupted. 'It burned down in 1803. It was a big E-shaped house with lots of plaster and wood. They're called Black and White houses! They were built like an E to honour Elizabeth the First.'

'So they were! What a knowledgeable young lady you are.' Mr Gilbey said. 'More importantly, it covered a large area and who knows what could be buried underneath that part of the garden?'

'But it will all be gone, if Mr Yates builds his houses!'

'No chance of that, my dear. We've found the long lost nephew and he arrives next week. Hill House is staying just the way it is!' Mr Forbes said, stabbing the plans with his finger.

Abigail was so pleased she jumped up and down, grabbing Jilly to jump for joy with her. They made the whole caravan shake!

'That's enough of that!' Mr Dutton laughed. 'We don't want to disappear down another hole, do we?'

'Don't we?' Mr Gilbey said, rubbing his hands at the thought of more discoveries, and everybody laughed.

Abigail stood at her bedroom window and looked across at Hill House. There were fairylights in the two tall ornamental firs that stood either side of the front doors, their colours reflected on the glistening white snow that lay over the lawns and flowerbeds. Behind the firs the windows were lit up, all of them and the house looked alive and loved.

It was Christmas and Abigail was dressed for a party in red leggings and a fluffy angora top, pure white like the snow outside. Jilly had promised to wear leggings and a top too, the last time she'd phoned.

Jilly was coming to stay with her grandparents for the holidays because her mum and dad were very busy. They were managing the hotel now and things were going really well.

It had begun to snow again as the Dutton family walked up the drive to Hill House. Daniel ran here and there to make the first footprints in the blanket of snow and Matthew made soft snowballs to throw at Nicola, Claire and Katie-Marie, who were walking behind.

Jilly was waiting at the coach house and after plenty of hugs and shaken hands, the guests joined Mr Lyle-Travis in the great marble hall of Hill House, restored to its former elegance.

There was music, games and Christmas food to follow, but first, after a welcoming drink of fruit punch, the party gathered in the little candle-lit church to celebrate the birth of Jesus and the beginnings of the Christian faith.

'I'm glad people don't have to hide any more,' Abigail whispered to Jilly.

'I'm glad we don't have to sneak through the rhododendrons!' Jilly grinned. 'But I'm sorry the summer house has gone!'

Abigail smiled, gazing at the little carved nativity scene, lit by candles in the niche in the back wall. Hill House was safe and loved again by Mr Lyle-Travis and his family – the gardens were carefully tended by a very happy Grandad – Mrs Potts was back in her kitchens and Jilly was back with her mum and dad.

Mr Dutton began to read the Christmas story from St Matthew's gospel and Abigail felt a warm glow inside. She had loving and forgiving parents that she could trust with any secret, with anything she was worried about. She would never keep anything from them again.

'The summer house has gone,' she whispered to Jilly, taking her hand and holding it tight. 'But we have so much more!'

Some other Leopard Books for you to read:

The Fiery Island
Sheila Spencer-Smith
To Lynette and Toby the island seems perfect. No one ever comes there. And it's a great place for sailing with Neil and Rowena. But when they discover intruders uprooting a rare plant and when their boat is rammed, they realise that both they and the island are in danger.

The Magic Kingdom
Cathie Bartlam
A free holiday in Florida! Emma can hardly believe that the family has been given the holiday of a lifetime.

For Emma and her brother Danny, who has cystic fibrosis, this trip to Disneyworld is the most exciting and fantastic experience – and for Emma it opens a doorway to a world even more wonderful.

The Moon-Piece
Pam Rowe
Brenig opened his hand and looked curiously at the small metal object that Marcus had given to him. It was a shining disc of a light coloured metal. As the light caught it, he could see the face of a

man. Was this the great moon god?

Brenig guards the 'moon-piece' carefully even when he is captured by the Romans, hoping it will bring him freedom.

Race to Anderloss
Lynette Bishop
If Alex's spaceship had been in working order he would have given up on the race, climbed back into the cockpit and let the ship take him back to civilization. He felt that his training had not prepared him for the ordeals of the race. And yet something drove him on, desperate to win.

Ring of Silver
Carol Hedges
The ring, which Nic finds on a building site, takes him back to Roman times where he meets Lucius. 'I am Lucius, the goldsmith.' The man held out his hand. 'Have you travelled far?'

Nic was baffled what to answer. 'From the twentieth cenury' would mean nothing at all to this man and might sound cheeky.

As Nic gets to know Lucius, the gap of centuries narrows, spanned by the Lord of time.

Expecting the Impossible
Christine Leonard
In this book you will meet eight people from around the world. They would say they were ordinary – yet they have all done extraordinary things. Some of them have been prepared to risk their lives doing what God has asked them to.

Read their exciting stories and think what God might do – through you!